Dear Brio Girl,

What if everything you believed in and held true exploded without warning? Foundations that were once so solid now seem to be made of sand, and nothing that was certain is sure anymore. When that happens, your world, and probably your faith, are rocked. Where will you find God?

Hannah's always been the unshakable one. Her principles and lifestyle testify to her sacrificial faith; troubles hit her friends, and Hannah reminds them of the Lord's perfect will. But when the unthinkable happens, Hannah's life and faith turn upside down.

The Brio gang is struggling with some hard questions, something I know you can relate to. I invite you to take this journey with them and continue your walk into a faith made real!

Your friend,

Susie Shellenberger, BRIO Editor
www.briomag.com

BRIO GIRLS®

from Focus on the Family®
and
Tyndale House Publishers, Inc.

brio girls®

REAL Faith MEETS REAL Life℠

Jacie Tyler Solana Becca

When Stars Fall

Created by

LISSA HALLS JOHNSON

WRITTEN BY KATHY WIERENGA BUCHANAN

TYNDALE

Tyndale House Publishers, Inc.
Wheaton, Illinois

When Stars Fall
by Kathy Wierenga Buchanan
Copyright © 2005
Focus on the Family

A Focus on the Family Book Published by Tyndale House Publishers, Wheaton,
Illinois 60189

Tyndale's quill logo is a trademark of Tyndale House Publishers, Inc.

BRIO GIRLS is a registered trademark of Focus on the Family.

Focus on the Family books are available at special quantity discounts when purchased in bulk by corporations, organizations, churches, or groups. Special
imprints, messages, and excerpts can be produced to meet your needs. For
more information, contact: Focus on the Family, 8605 Explorer Drive, Colorado
Springs, CO 80920; phone (800) 932-9123.

Library of Congress Cataloging-in-Publication Data
Wierenga Buchanan, Kathy.
  When stars fall / created by Lissa Halls Johnson; written by Kathy Wierenga
Buchanan.
     p. cm. — (Brio girls (Tyndale House Publishers))
  "Focus on the family."
  Summary: Overwhelmed by a series of tragedies, Hannah is distressed to find that
she no longer has all the answers and is not sure that God does either, making her
unable to bolster her friends' faith or cope with her own grief.
  ISBN 1-58997-090-X
  [1. Trust in God—Fiction. 2. Faith—Fiction. 3. Interpersonal relations—Fiction. 4.
High schools—Fiction. 5. Schools—Fiction. 6. Christian life—Fiction.] I. Johnson,
Lissa Halls, 1955- II. Title. III. Series.

PZ7.W63583Wh 2005
[Fic]—dc22   2004021638

Editor: Lissa Halls Johnson
Cover design by Lookout Design Group, Inc.

Printed in the United States of America

To Phil Lollar,
for believing that I could write.

To Al Janssen,
for giving me the chance.

And to Lissa Halls Johnson,
for being a wonderful editor, encouraging coach, and dear friend.

KATHY WIERENGA BUCHANAN resides in Colorado Springs where she loves spending time with her husband, Sean, and their baby girl. She's on staff at Focus on the Family as a writer and director for the children's radio show, ADVENTURES IN ODYSSEY® and enjoys writing for the BRIO series too. She received her Bachelor's degree from Taylor University and a Master's degree in Biblical Counseling from Colorado Christian University. Kathy is passionate about hiking the mountains, traveling around Italy and, most of all, knowing God intimately and continuing to experience His redemption in her life.

chapter 1

Festinate: *To hurry, to speed.*

I festinate through dinner when I'm very hungry.

Lassitude: *A state or feeling of being tired and listless; weariness, languor.*

My attitude toward life is characterized by lassitude.

Pentadactyl: *Having five fingers or toes on each hand or foot.*

I'm very happy to be a pentadactyl creature.

Hannah put down her vocabulary sheet. She knew all the words. She'd studied them last night. Sometimes words had silly definitions, like the description was too fancy to really help you understand what the word really meant. But *lassitude* stuck with her. That's how she felt. She pulled out her journal.

I wonder if I'm doing enough. It kind of seems like a silly question to ask. I mean the Brio gang and I just went through this whole thing with Becca doing too much. She needed to slow down. But this is different. I have enough activities on my plate. Church orchestra, newspaper photographer, my running. But . . . I feel like everything I'm doing is for me, even hanging out with my friends. I do it because I like it, not because it's a ministry of any kind. Shouldn't I always be involved in some sort of ministry, God? Isn't that why You made me? Aunt Dinah's leaving on a missions trip to Kenya next week. My parents are volunteering at the Pregnancy Center. Even Jacie and Tyler are helping out with leadership for The Edge. But me? I'm not doing anything. At least . . . nothing that makes a difference. Maybe that's what I should focus on this school year: finding where You're calling me to work, what You want me to do.

Hannah leaned back against her pillows and reread what she'd written, half hoping God's hand would come down from heaven and write personal directions on the bottom half of her journal entry. She closed her eyes.

What is it, God? What is it?

A tiny tickle touched her cheek.

Was that God?

No, just a drip from her still-wet hair wrapped in a towel turban-style. No answers yet. She should get ready for school.

"Hannah!" Mrs. Connor's voice traveled up to Hannah's attic bedroom. "Jacie's on the phone."

Hope she's not sick, Hannah thought as she flopped her journal closed and hurried down the stairs. Jacie always picked her up for school, so she'd call if she couldn't make it.

"Hi, Jacie. Are you okay?"

"I am, but Solana's not."

"What's wrong?"

"I don't know, but she sounded like she was crying on the phone. She wants us to meet at Alyeria before school. Are you almost ready?"

"Sure." She'd throw on a sweater and a khaki skirt, pull her hair back into a ponytail, and be set.

"I'll be there in 10 minutes," Jacie said.

I'll need to hurry, thought Hannah as she raced back upstairs, *or should I say, festinate.*

Although a part of Hannah's heart felt concern for Solana, another part of her relished the thought that she really belonged to the *Brio* group. She'd come into their friendship circle as an outsider. Tyler, Solana, Becca, and Jacie had been friends since grade school. The core of the foursome's friendship lay in an aspen grove just inside the elementary school playground where they'd played as children. Now they met there when one of the group members really needed to talk. *Alyeria* they'd named it. It was a sacred spot, but a place where Hannah was now welcomed. *I'm really a part of the group.*

She caught sight of the journal. Maybe that's how God would use her this year. He might have introduced her to this group of friends so she could encourage them in their spiritual walks. They were all Christians with the exception of Solana. And maybe He would even use her to bring Solana into the kingdom. The idea excited her. She tugged a pink cable-knit sweater over her head. *Wouldn't that be the perfect end to our senior year if Solana came to know the Lord? And Tyler, Becca, and Jacie all had strengthened faith because of my input?* What a great purpose.

She forced a comb through her wet, blonde locks and examined herself in the tiny mirror that hung above her dresser. Cornflower blue eyes framed with thick, dark lashes stared back at her. *God, help me to do this well,* she prayed. *Help me see the opportunities You give me to speak truth to my friends.*

She stuck her vocab sheet in her backpack just as Jacie's horn beeped in the driveway. She had her own definition for the word that popped into her head.

Purpose: *Knowing why God put you on earth.*

● ● ●

The sun was still making its appearance while Jacie and Hannah drove to Copper Ridge Elementary School. Pink clouds piled in the sky like a fluff of cotton candy off its cardboard stick.

"What do you think it is?" Jacie asked.

It took Hannah a second to realize Jacie was referring to Solana's problem.

"The only thing I can think of I hope desperately that it's not."

"What's that?"

"I'm afraid she slept with Ramón again."

Jacie's hands tightened on the steering wheel. "I can't imagine she'd do that, though. I mean, Solana is disciplined, if anything. And when she makes a decision, she sticks with it. After last time, she knew she didn't want to—"

"But hasn't Ramón broken *all* of Solana's rules?"

It was true. Solana had given up dating entirely before Ramón walked—or, rather, rode his horse—into her life. It was the one time Hannah had seen Solana vulnerable and emotional and completely smitten. She'd walked on air. And then she crashed after they'd had sex. The two had decided to call off the relationship to try to reverse the damage they'd done to themselves. But the chemistry pervaded, and they still wanted to be together. So they'd gone back to dating. Anyone within a mile could tell the sparks were flying. Solana still held out hope that she and Ramón would someday be together.

Hannah hated that Solana didn't think there would be any future consequences over her having had sex outside of marriage. Solana felt bad about her choices and didn't want to go there again, but she thought a person would just get over it and then have a perfectly healthy and happy relationship. Didn't she know how untrue this was? What if she *had* made the same mistake? Hannah would stand by Solana, of course. They all would.

Jacie tapped her fingers along the steering wheel, while a commercial citing the benefits of Ben-Gay over other muscle creams played on the radio.

Hannah's mind went to work. She'd comfort Solana, remind her that she was created in the image of God whether she believed it or not. She'd tell her there could be another way. If Solana would just listen . . .

"Do you think she regrets it?" Hannah asked.

"From the way she sounded on the phone, whatever she's going to tell us isn't good news." Jacie pulled into the dirt alongside the road. The grove was just down the slope. She pulled the keys from the ignition, silencing the weatherman. "Hannah, please don't say anything—" she paused, "anything rash."

"Rash?" Hannah repeated. "You know I love Solana." Her heart beat a little faster. Was she being judgmental again?

"I know you do. But sometimes you can get 'preachy.'" Jacie rushed on as though to cover the sting of the word. "I know you mean well, and you just want to help. And like the rest of us you want to be a good witness to Solana." She took a deep breath. "But I think sometimes it's more hurtful than it is helpful."

"I don't mean for it to be." This wasn't the first time one of the *Brio* friends had expressed to Hannah that she could be more lecturing than understanding. She tried—she really did— to not overdo it, but sometimes it was hard. *After all, didn't Christ call us to speak truth?* What was the balance of showing love and telling people the "right" way? She was learning, but she still had a long way to go.

● ● ●

The news wasn't at all what Hannah—or anyone—had expected.

"Ramón and I aren't going to see each other anymore. He's moving," Solana said, sitting on a fallen tree, her legs out-stretched.

Becca, Jacie, Tyler, and Hannah sat circled around her.

"What? Where?" Becca asked.

Solana explained the story. Ramón had received a job at MIT—the school he'd been planning to attend next year, after a second year of junior college. He hadn't thought he could afford to go this soon, but with a new research fellowship, he'd be able to go to school for free and get great experience working in the laboratory. It was too good of an opportunity to pass up.

"So when we talked last night, he told me he didn't think we should continue officially dating. He said he didn't want to tie me down. Long-distance relationships are too hard. All the stuff I know," Solana sniffed, "but nothing that I wanted to apply to us."

"Did you tell him that?" asked Jacie.

"Sort of. I mean, I don't want to beg him to stay with me. I'd just hoped he'd want to. But what he says makes sense. I can't fault him for that. He says if we're meant to be together it will all come back around." Solana kicked a stone, sending it skidding across the grove. "Maybe he's right, but I wish he didn't have to leave."

The rest of the gang nodded sympathetically. They all knew how much Ramón meant to Solana.

"When is he leaving?" asked Tyler.

"Tomorrow. The school even got him a plane ticket. Apparently someone backed out at the last minute and they need him there right away."

Hannah knew Solana was on the verge of tears, but she'd control it. She always did.

Solana continued. "He's spending time with his family tonight. He said I could come over and say good-bye, but he didn't want me to stay long. He said it would be too hard. I don't even know if I should go." Solana thumped her foot against the white trunk of an aspen tree, shimmying its yellow leaves and causing some to break loose.

"Will you stay in touch with him?" asked Becca.

"Yeah, I hope. But I know what's going to happen. He'll meet all these girls in his classes. Girls that have the same interests and passions he does—like I do, but they'll be closer. And they'll swarm around him like gnats. He'll forget about me in a nanosecond."

"You know that's not true," Jacie said. "Ramón cares about you a lot."

"Distance does weird things, though," Solana said. Hannah watched Jacie's head drop. She knew what Solana said was true. Jacie's dad lived in California and, as much as he cared for Jacie, it was no secret Bennett Crosse lacked the understanding and emotional closeness of a parent who lived close by. Even Hannah could relate to what Solana said. She'd left her friends in Michigan, and rarely thought of them now.

Tyler wrapped his arm around Solana's shoulders. "This stinks, Sol. I'm really sorry."

"It feels like someone died, like I lost the one person in my life who understood me. I mean," she corrected herself, "you guys know me, but with Ramón it was . . . different."

Hannah knew what Solana wasn't saying. Ramón was the only one who understood why Solana didn't want to become a Christian. The rest of the *Brio* group had committed their lives to Christ and chosen to live out their faith. Solana was as much a part of the group as anyone else, but her beliefs were very different. And Ramón had understood that part of her while the others couldn't. More than that, their minds and insatiable desire to understand science were so equally matched. Hannah had to admit that aside from their wrong physical involvement, they had a relationship a lot of people never achieve.

Solana wiped the wetness from her eyes with the edge of her jacket. "This is silly. I'm not going to be crying over some guy who doesn't want me."

"It's okay to feel sad," Tyler said.

Hannah had always been impressed with Tyler's sensitivity. With his sun-streaked blond hair and athletic build, he'd been labeled quite the catch at school, but thankfully, his heart still outgrew his head. Or, perhaps it was as Solana said—he'd had too many surfboard blows while riding the waves in California to notice the girls at school who fawned over him.

Solana looked up at the quaking branches dancing in the wind. She paused for a moment. "I have to be logical about it, though. Ramón's reasons make sense. And it won't do me any good to cry about it."

Hannah sat back on a log and played with the long strands

of grass. *So like Solana*, she thought. *Determined and logical and strong. Maybe that's why she can't see the need of knowing Christ. She can't stand the thought of handing the reins of her life to someone else.* Whereas most girls would be devastated that the man they'd lost their virginity to had abandoned them, Solana would attempt to treat it as just another occurrence in life that she could choose to move past.

Hannah twisted her fingers into little knots on her lap. She didn't know what to say. Given the worries she'd had about Solana and Ramón on the way here, wasn't this almost good news? Maybe this was God's way of getting rid of someone who would keep Solana from becoming a Christian. Didn't God do everything for a purpose? Solana wouldn't understand that, but maybe, in time, Hannah could show her this was all for the best. She watched silently as her other friends mulled over their own confusion and "what do we do now?" thoughts. Were they thinking the same thing she was?

Jacie stroked Solana's back, while Becca awkwardly patted her knee.

Tyler glanced at his watch. "It's 10 'til. We better get going."

● ● ●

"What's that poking out of your locker, Hannah?" Jacie asked.

Hannah squinted through the crowd of people pushing their way down the halls at Stony Brook High. Sure enough, a lavender piece of paper seemed to be stuffed through the locker vents. Hannah's heart did an involuntary leap. *Another note?* She fumbled through her combination. "I don't know. Maybe an assignment fell out of my history book."

"Yeah," smirked Solana. "Mrs. Porter always gives assignments on lavender stationery."

"Maybe it's a lo-ove note," said Becca. She swooned overdramatically. "From your secret admirer."

Hannah's heart skipped a beat. Her secret admirer had come into the picture last spring, occasionally leaving notes or surprising Hannah with flowers. The group hadn't a clue who the mysterious devotee could be, but they never tired of teasing Hannah about him. After all, how ironic that the girl who'd determined to not have love interests at this stage in her life would be the one being chased after with romantic intent.

"It could be hate mail, too," mused Solana. "Maybe a death threat. Now that would be cool. We haven't had a death threat around here in a while."

Hannah unfolded the paper and skimmed its contents. *Oh, wow.* "It is!"

"A death threat?" Jacie asked, wide-eyed.

"No," Hannah said. The neatly printed words popped off the page.

Couldn't help but notice your lovely smile.
Your eyes that put the sky to shame.
Your soft, sweet words.
Just to let you know someone you don't know is thinking of you.

Hannah stifled a silly-girl giggle. "I think it's a love note."

chapter 2

"Definitely a guy's handwriting," Solana stated.

"Well, that's a relief," Jacie said.

Solana ignored Jacie's sarcasm. "It's pretty stationery, so we're not talking about a jock."

"Hey," argued Becca, "as a jock, I'm offended by that. Athletes know how to spell these days, and yes, we can even be sensitive. Right, Tyler?"

"Sure. Although, speaking as a *male* jock, I don't have purple stationery."

"Lavender," the four girls corrected him.

"Whatever."

"And he must be romantic," Becca said.

"I'm guessing a good English student," Jacie added.

"And . . . hmmm . . . 'someone you don't know.' Does that mean someone you've never met?" wondered Solana.

"Or is he just referring to the fact that you don't know who sent it?" said Tyler.

"He's been close enough to see your eyes, apparently," said Becca.

"Unless that's just romantic wording," said Jacie.

"He has to know they're blue because he compared them to the sky," said Solana.

"Good point," agreed Jacie.

"So are we assuming this is the same guy who sent the roses on the ski trip and left the flowers and candy on your car a while ago?" Jacie said.

"My guess would be yes," said Solana.

Hannah thought so too. And even though it must be wrong to enjoy it so much, the attention was flattering. She smiled, thinking how wonderful it was that someone liked *her*. Could she enjoy someone's interest in her without going against her courtship vow?

"Doesn't this drive you crazy, Hannah?" asked Becca. "I think I'm more interested in who it is than you are."

Hannah laughed, but she knew it wasn't true. She slid her fingers against the edge of the stationery, a small smile playing on her lips. Who could this boy be? The only thing she knew about him was that he was sweet and romantic and obviously liked her a lot. She never said it out loud—not even out loud in her head—but she was dying to know who he was. Sometimes she dreamed about this faceless boy at night speaking the words on the notes to her. But, at the same time, she was scared to find out his identity. Because once she knew, she'd be obligated to have the "I can't date, I choose courtship" conversation she'd had with other boys many times before. She hadn't been inter-ested in them, so the tedious conversation proved to be a con-venient excuse. But this time, it would mean the end of the surprise, the little thrilling trill of her heart as she unfolded a note to see what this unknown Romeo thought of her. And, much as she hated to admit it, she loved that feeling. She felt a blush coming on, so she busied herself by collecting her books for her first class.

Solana handed Tyler a pen. "Here, Tyler, write 'Couldn't help but notice your lovely smile.'"

"Why?"

"No reason." Solana blinked innocently.

"You think *I* wrote the note?"

"Well, I need to start eliminating somewhere."

Jacie snatched the note. "It's not Ty's handwriting. Not even close."

Tyler gave a good-natured wink. "Besides, I've learned my Hannah lesson."

Hannah's cheeks pinked, as she slammed her locker shut. She'd rather not remember that horrible ski trip when she ended up kissing two boys after promising herself—and, worse, promising God—she wouldn't kiss until she met the man she was to marry. It all ended up okay but still ranked up there with her most humiliating moments.

"For not believing in dating, you certainly have quite the reputation," Solana said.

"Hannah has one of the best reputations at this school," Jacie reminded her. The *Brio* amoeba made their way down the crowded hallway.

"If you equate purest with best. But not all of us do," Solana said. "It's just so odd."

"What's odd? Hannah's secret admirer?" Jacie asked.

"That there are so many guys after Hannah. I mean, you're cute and all, Hannah, but why would guys go gaga over the Courtship Queen?"

Hannah had a mixed reputation of being wholesomely kind and prudishly old-fashioned. But Hannah didn't care—at least, not much. Committed to her Christian walk, she enjoyed taking the "high road"—something her other friends didn't always understand but accepted about her.

She'd never cared much about being popular—as long as she had a few good friends. That's what her Aunt Dinah had recommended a long time ago.

"Hannah," her pretty aunt had said, "I went through my high school career trying to be the most popular girl there. Went to all the right parties, dated all the right guys, dressed in all the right looks—and then I found out I was pregnant and had . . . nothing. Not even one friend who *really* knew me, who I could be authentic with, and who would stand by me. It all became an act, and *I* didn't even know who I was. Now I'd take one honest, good friend over a thousand admirers."

Her aunt, a surprise little sister on her dad's side, was only 14 years older than Hannah. But she was a world wiser. That reminded her . . . .

"Aunt Dinah is going to be in town today and wanted to have coffee with us after school. Are you guys up for it?"

"Sure, I love your aunt," Becca said.

"Me, too," Solana said. "Which is funny. Because the first time you talked about her being your role model, I thought she'd be too stuffy to like." Hannah remembered. Dinah had come early to the coffee shop and was waiting when Solana showed up before the others. The two had struck up a conversation, and not knowing this was Hannah's beloved aunt, Solana talked Dinah's ear off about how she wasn't looking forward to meeting her friend's frumpy old aunt but felt she should as a pal. Dinah kept a straight face for almost five minutes, and then about died laughing.

"I'll be there," Tyler said.

"Count me in, too," Jacie added. "How's her pregnancy going?"

"Pretty well, I think. She's so excited about it," Hannah

said. She was excited about it, too. A cute little baby to hold and cuddle and play with would be so much fun. She'd been around babies her entire life, and now that the twins were five, she missed it. "I can't wait to see how pregnant she looks—"

The shrill ring of the first bell cut off Hannah's sentence, and the group said hurried good-byes and rushed off to class. Hannah stood outside her chemistry class for a minute, smoothing her hands over the note she still clutched. *Who in the world could it be from?*

● ● ●

Friendship: *Knowing that another person's fries are just as much yours as theirs.*

Becca, Tyler, and Hannah sat picking at Jacie's plate of fries at their usual cafeteria table.

Solana set down her lunch tray with a thump, sloshing milk over the edges of the open carton. "I've made a decision."

"What is it?" Hannah asked, wiping some extra ketchup off her lip. She hoped Solana wasn't going to hop on a bus and chase after Ramón. The more she thought about the conversation at the grove this morning, the more she believed this was God's way of keeping Solana away from an unhealthy relationship. And she had determined to do anything to help make that happen.

"I'm over Ramón."

The four friends stared at her, skepticism written on their faces.

"I mean it. We were talking today in biology about bees. And I've decided I want to be a queen bee."

"Ummm . . . don't you need to have wings to do that?" Becca asked.

"And buzz?" added Tyler. He stuffed another fry in his mouth.

Solana rolled her eyes. "Just listen, science morons. The queen's got it all. She's in control. She mates with other bees, she runs the hive, she has bees-in-waiting taking care of her. She has no emotional attachments."

"Doesn't she also just give birth over and over and over again?" Jacie said.

Solana shook her head. "That's beside the point. So I'm sitting here and listening in bio thinking: I have two choices. I can either wallow in feeling crummy about Ramón, or I can go on with life. And, c'mon, I'm a senior in high school—the prime of my life. Why not date around?"

"Because you tried that and realized there was no one worth dating," Becca reminded her.

"Especially when you have friends like us to spend time with," said Jacie.

"But dating is fun! And isn't that what being a senior is all about? Having fun?" Solana threw up her hands to emphasize her point.

Hannah let Solana's words soak in. If dating would keep Solana's mind off Ramón, it could be a good thing. *Because then she'd realize the futility of dating around, and by the end of the year, all she'd have left is to know God.* Okay . . . it was kind of a stretch, but God could do anything, right?

Solana broke into Hannah's thoughts. "I suppose now you're going to give me a lecture on how dating will ruin me?"

Hannah shrugged. "No. I think it might be a good idea."

She almost enjoyed the sight of four jaws dropping around her.

"What? You agree?" asked Becca.

"It could be good for her," Hannah said.

"Just the fact that you approve makes me want to question it. But I'll bypass that for now. Ladies and Gentleman, Solana

Luz is back on the prowl. There isn't a safe man at Stony Brook High." She raised her fist in the air.

"You're scaring me," Tyler said.

"And I know exactly what I'm going to do," Solana said, grabbing a greasy fry off her plate and shoving it into her mouth. "I've developed a dating hypothesis."

"Oh, boy. Did you even pay attention in biology?" asked Becca.

"All stuff I knew already." Solana chewed and swallowed. "So are you ready to hear it? I call it the Hannah Connor Theory."

Hannah's grip loosened on her sandwich, and her tomato slid out onto the table.

Solana's dark eyes danced. "It's a theory on why so many guys are interested in Hannah."

"Sure. She's got a great body," Tyler said. There was a pause of silence as the girls turned to stare at him. He slapped his hand over his mouth. "Did I say that out loud?" he squeaked.

Hannah blushed. She didn't want to think about her body that way. Did guys really think so? She had always tried to hide her curves as much as possible. Maybe she wasn't trying hard enough. She couldn't think about that right now. She was more interested in moving past Tyler's comment as quickly as possible. She gave Solana her full attention. "What made you decide to theorize about my life?"

"Because I was thinking. Y'know how before I met Ramón I gave up dating because I was so sick of how immature all the guys we knew were?" The group nodded. Except Tyler, who cleared his throat.

"Right, Ty. With a comment like that last one?" said Solana.

"Point taken," said Tyler.

"But then it seemed like guys were popping out of the woodwork to ask me out."

"Like Ramón," said Becca.

"Exactly. And then after that whole mess, I gave up dating again, right? And once more, I'm barraged with male attention. Guys always want what they can't have, so if they think they can't have me, they want me."

"Tyler, is that hard-to-get stuff really true?" asked Becca.

Tyler shrugged and didn't look up. "Sometimes, I guess."

Hannah remembered when Tyler had a crush on her. Had it only been because she'd been unattainable? The idea felt disturbing. She'd thought maybe it was because he really liked who she was.

"I think it has to do with their primitive hunting nature—" Solana continued.

"Oh, here we go," Becca said.

"Men like the adventure of the hunt. The challenge. The idea of conquering something." Solana put another greasy fry into her mouth.

Tyler pounded on his chest. "I am man. Hear me roar."

"You're not helping, surfer-caveman. Anyway, so once the deer is shot, the bear is captured, the fish is caught, what's the point? They'll just move on to a bigger challenge."

"So how do you explain 50-year marriages?" Hannah asked.

Solana's eyebrows raised. "Uh . . . good question. Maybe guys eventually outgrow the caveman stage."

"Or they just get too tired." Tyler grunted, "Chasing women tough work for caveman."

Solana pretended to ignore him. "So the theory is this: The more unattainable you are, the more people want to attain you."

"Interesting," said Becca.

"Profound," Jacie said.

"Quite likely," Tyler added.

"Pathetic," Hannah said. "You're treating relationships like your scientific theorems."

"That's exactly what it is. So, now the next step is to test the hypothesis in a controlled environment."

"And who might your lab rat be?" Tyler quipped.

"Galvin Parker. Although let's refer to him as the test subject."

"Very well."

"Who's Galvin Parker?" asked Hannah.

Solana rolled her eyes. "Okay. You're just freaky. It's one thing to not date. It's another thing to not even realize there is an incredibly hot new guy in school this year."

"I'm sure I'm not the only one who missed it," Hannah defended herself. She turned to Becca and Jacie. "Do you know who she's talking about?"

"Absolutely," Jacie said.

"Without question," Becca added.

"Even I noticed him," Tyler said.

The girls looked at him, amused.

"Not like that! I just wondered if he was a basketball player. He's tall."

"Anyway, how do you plan on conducting the experiment?" Jacie asked.

"Well, I've seen a lot of other girls very interested in him—flirting, laughing at his jokes, catching his eye—y'know, all the tricks. Hardly a response. So I'm going to be very *uninterested*, and see if that changes his mind."

"Doesn't a controlled experiment mean that there aren't any other variables?" asked Jacie.

"What's the variable?" Solana asked.

"Kassidy Jordan." Jacie nodded her head toward a table in the corner.

Hannah turned along with everyone else. A tall, attractive

guy—whom Hannah guessed must be Galvin—sat surrounded by the tight-jean group of girls, of which the ringleader was always-tanned, tiny-waisted, wavy blonde-haired Kassidy Jordan. All the girls wore bright lipstick and tight, tight jeans— hence their name, the "tight-jean girls." And Kassidy was the tight-jean queen. She always got her man. For a long time in junior high, Hannah had heard, Solana and Kassidy would end up in spats over the same guy. But their tastes seemed to have changed in high school. Kassidy went for the wild party guys. And Solana was more interested in the intelligent, non-druggie type. But it looked like their tastes may have circled around and landed on the same poor, unassuming Galvin Parker.

Hannah looked up to see Solana's expression. Her mouth was set tight, and her eyes narrowed. "One small variable," Solana agreed. "But that doesn't make the experiment undoable." She smiled a slow smile. "It merely makes it more interesting."

chapter 3

The warmth of the coffee shop enveloped Hannah as soon as she walked through the door. A little wood-burning stove in the corner contained crackling orange flames. Dark woods and fuzzy carpets added to the atmosphere. Three empty over-stuffed chairs faced a brown leather love seat, piled high with pillows. An oak coffee table sat in the center of them all. It was where they always sat, the five of them. With Dinah, they would have to squeeze three onto the love seat, making it even more cozy.

She looked around the shop, noticing a table of guys from her English class. One of them waved in her direction, and she nodded a reply before scanning the other faces for her aunt. She caught sight of a platinum blonde shot of hair at the counter. Dinah stood with her back facing the door, talking animatedly to the guy behind the counter.

"Dinah," Hannah squealed, hugging her aunt from behind.

"Hi, sweetie!" Dinah turned and returned the hug. "It is so good to see you! I was just having a very interesting conversation about the apocalypse." She smiled at the young man behind the counter.

"Hi, Hannah," the guy said. "Your aunt sure knows her stuff."

"Hi," Hannah said. She knew she should know the server's name, but she was always forgetting things like that. "Yeah, she knows a lot."

"I'd better spend some time with my favorite niece," Dinah said. "Maybe we'll have time to talk again." She smiled one of her gigantic genuine smiles at him.

Hannah wanted to shake her head. Her aunt made easy friendships everywhere she went. "Is anyone a stranger to you?" she asked as the two walked over to the couches.

Dinah smiled. "People are fascinating, Hannah. You should let yourself connect with people like Grant," she said, indicating the guy behind the counter.

Grant. I've got to remember that.

"I hate talking to guys."

"That's what I'm telling you. You need to let more people into your life. You'll find they're fascinating."

"If I talk to them they think I like them."

Dinah sighed as she lowered herself into the sofa. "But you're missing out on so much."

Hannah wanted to change the subject. "You always get here early. How come?"

"To be sure not to miss one moment with you," Dinah said. "Is the rest of the gang coming?"

"They should be here any minute." She looked down at Aunt Dinah's round belly. "You look great."

"I look fat, but thank you."

Hannah had been thrilled when her aunt had told her family

a couple months ago that she and Greg were expecting a baby. Always a world traveler who got antsy when life became routine, Dinah didn't seem the type who would ever fall in love and settle down. But when she fell in love, she fell hard. And, after meeting Greg, the youth pastor at Dinah's church, Hannah understood why. Now here she was, married and pregnant. How quickly life could change.

"We found out yesterday that the baby is a girl," Dinah grinned.

"A little girl! How precious!" Hannah squealed. "And you said you were kind of hoping for a girl."

"I just had a feeling."

"Have you thought up names yet?"

"We've been talking about it for months, and I think we've settled on McKenzie Joy. McKenzie means 'Favored One.' What do you think?"

"McKenzie Joy." Hannah let the name roll off her tongue. "I love it."

"Well, then get used to it," Dinah said.

"How does Greg feel about it?" Hannah asked.

"He's so excited. He's just so overwhelmed with planning this trip right now. I can't believe we're leaving next week."

"Kenya. I'm so jealous," Hannah said.

Dinah smiled. "I just love how God worked it out."

Hannah knew what she meant. Her aunt had always expressed a burden for the Kenyan people. She'd traveled there often with her previous pharmaceutical job, and she knew the country inside and out. So when the youth group that Greg pastored begged her to take them on a missions trip there, nothing could have thrilled her more. The trip would focus on medical missions, with the teens working in a health-care facility. Dinah would be providing the doctors new drugs and teaching them how to administer the medications.

"Our Father is so amazing," Dinah continued, taking a sip of her tea. "He's using the youth group, and my job in pharmaceuticals, and the connections I have with different companies to do something so life-changing for the local people as well as for the kids. It couldn't be more perfect."

"You must be so excited," Hannah said. She remembered her own thoughts earlier of God not using her for anything. Why couldn't God use her like He did Dinah? She remembered her own frustrating missions trip to Venezuela. So much she could have done, but she kept blowing it. She wished she could go on this trip with Dinah. She'd be sure to do it right this time.

"I'm itching to go back to Kenya. But," she pointed a finger at Hannah, "you need to remember to pray for me. I know my way around, but I've never led 20 teenagers. I only had to worry about myself. I'm nervous one of them will get hurt, or we'll lose one." She absentmindedly rubbed her swollen belly.

"It's a good thing Greg's the responsible one."

"Yeah," Dinah laughed. "But enough about me; what's going on with you?"

Hannah sighed, embarrassed at her answer. "Nothing. That's the whole point. My life is purposeless."

"I find that a little hard to believe."

"It's true. You wouldn't understand. You're doing missions trips and changing people's lives and all kinds of great things for God. I'm just going to school, being a teenager." Hannah felt whiney, but she didn't care.

"Well, you're much better at being a teenager than I was, at least," Dinah said.

"But you weren't a Christian when you got into all your trouble. I am a Christian and I'm not doing a single good thing. God should be using me to do something, shouldn't He?"

"Maybe He is, in ways you don't expect."

"It doesn't feel that way."

"Or maybe He's growing your character. The Christian life isn't always about doing stuff for God. There are times when we're not *doing*, we're *growing*."

Hannah hadn't thought of that.

Dinah put her hand on Hannah's. "I have a feeling that God uses you even in the words you give your friends." The opening door distracted her momentarily. "Looks like everyone but Solana's here!"

Tyler, Becca, and Jacie tumbled in the front door of the coffee shop.

"Hi, Dinah," they chorused.

"Where's Solana?" Dinah asked after they'd all exchanged hugs and greetings.

"Coming later," Becca said.

Tyler stood up. "What can I get everyone? Hot tea for Hannah. Jacie, what kind of latte are you up for?"

"Feels like a raspberry day to me," Jacie said.

"Water for me, please," Becca said.

"Well, aren't you the healthy one?" Dinah said.

"Basketball season. And it's going to be the best one yet. I'm co-captain this year."

"Congratulations, that's great," Dinah said.

Becca continued talking about her excitement over the coming season. Hannah phased out. She'd never really understood picks, fouls, and key rules. Once Becca had mentioned she'd been penalized for traveling, and Hannah had thought it was because Becca and her family had gone on vacation the previous week. Eventually, Becca got frustrated and gave up trying to explain it all.

"Do you think you'll play in college?" Dinah asked.

Becca made a face. "Don't remind me about next year. I'm so far behind in my applications," she groaned.

"It's kind of a sore subject, Dinah," Jacie explained. "Except for Solana, we're all unsure of where we're going to school, but the pressure is on to decide. I've got it narrowed down—to 11 schools."

"It's a huge decision," Dinah acknowledged.

"I've thought about Wheaton, where my brother goes," said Becca. "But more and more I think I want to start my own McKinnon identity somewhere—but I don't know where. Maybe California. Or Washington State. Or Hawaii."

Tyler returned from placing the drink order. "I know where I'm going."

"University of Colorado in Boulder," Jacie, Becca, and Hannah said in unison. Tyler had been talking about it for years, and even more so these last few months.

Hannah had applied to a few schools, mostly small Christian colleges. But she too was uncertain as to where God was leading her. And right now she didn't even want to think about it. She loved her friends and had grown closer to them in the past year than any group of friends she'd ever had. The idea of them all going their separate ways made her stomach turn.

She looked around the circle. She thought of all the conversations that had taken place here. The group gathered over their drinks as they discussed Tyler's girl problems, Jacie's artwork, Solana's injured uncle, Becca and Nate's relationship. Here they had deep conversations and fun interactions. These chairs had heard a lot of laughter. *I'm so blessed, God.* Minus her parents and siblings, the people she cared about most in this world were seated right here. *Except where was . . . ?*

"Yowzers, it's cold out there." Solana stepped inside the coffee shop, a scattering of leaves chasing after her. "Could you get me a caramel mocha, Grant?"

"You bet."

"Well, no wonder you're cold, Sol," laughed Tyler. "Look at what you're wearing."

Solana sported a plunging V-neck top and denim miniskirt under a thin suede jacket.

"I know perfectly well what I'm wearing," snapped Solana. "I hate wearing layers of clothes. It feels so . . . bunchy." She grinned at Aunt Dinah and leaned down to give her a hug. "Hey, Dinah!"

"Well, I've got news for all of you." Solana plopped herself down on one of the Copperchino's large overstuffed chairs.

"Let me guess." Becca leaned forward. "You're switching from Siren Red lipstick to Cranberry Splash."

"Oh, you're so funny. I mean I started testing my theory."

"On Galvin?" asked Jacie.

"This you have to tell me about," Dinah cut in.

The *Brio* gang quickly explained their conversation earlier that day.

"And so as he was leaving school today, I purposely stayed at my locker. Kassidy Jordan was a few feet away waiting for him. Galvin saunters by in that oh-so-sexy saunter of his and Kassidy goes . . ." Solana turned her voice sultry, "Hi, Galvin."

"And you slugged her?" Becca said.

"Nope, I just continued to pretend to look for a book. So Galvin says hi back, and she starts asking what he's doing after school—maybe he'd like to go hang out with a bunch of them at Crazy Charlie's. And he says—get this—'No, thanks.'"

"Nothing else?" asked Jacie.

"That was it." Solana grinned triumphantly.

"Bye, bye, Kassidy," said Tyler.

"He said, 'No, thanks.' That doesn't mean he doesn't like her," Hannah argued. "Maybe he just had homework to do."

"No way. That's a definite 'I'm-not-interested-get-outta-my-way' response," said Becca.

Jacie nodded in agreement. "First of all, homework can always wait, but even if he *did* have something else he had to do but wanted to go, he'd have made that very clear."

"Crystal," added Tyler. "Like 'Wow, that sounds cool, but I'm late for my shift at work. Can I catch you tomorrow?' That's what he would have said."

"Sounds like you've had some practice, Ty," said Becca.

"I've had to turn down a few women in my life," Tyler stretched back in his chair. "Or beat them away with a stick."

Hannah wanted someone else on her side. "Aunt Dinah, that wasn't necessarily a turndown, was it?"

"Oh, absolutely it was," Dinah said.

"Okay, okay," Solana urged the attention back onto herself. "I haven't even told you the good part yet! After he says, 'No, thanks' to Kassidy, he turns around toward me and says, 'Bye, Solana!'"

"No way! And you never said anything to him?" Becca said.

"Didn't even throw a glance his direction."

"What did you do after he said bye to you?" Jacie asked.

"Just a small smile. Less than an 'I'm interested' smile, but more than a 'forced smile.' And I said, 'See you later.'"

"Oooh, you are good." Tyler gave Solana a high five.

"Here you go, guys." Froth-filled mugs clinked together as the coffee guy placed them on the rustic wooden coffee table in the middle of the group. "Can I get you anything else?"

"Um . . . yes," Hannah said. She wanted honey, but she was embarrassed because she already couldn't remember the name of the guy. Dinah said his name just moments ago. So did Solana. Why couldn't she remember his name? Maybe because she always thought of him as the coffee guy. "Do you have honey?"

"I already put it in there for you." The lanky boy grinned. "Let me know if it's okay. I can get you more."

Hannah took a sip. "Mmm. It's perfect. Thanks."

"Good."

"Okay everyone, pay up." Tyler reached for his wallet.

"Oh, no, no," said Dinah. "This is my treat." She handed the coffee guy her credit card.

"I'll put five drinks on it, but Hannah's was already bought by someone else."

Hannah's eyebrows arched. "Who?"

"Some guy who was in here earlier." Coffee guy headed back to the counter.

"Who was in here when you walked in? Think, think," said Solana.

Hannah tried to remember. "I don't know. There were two little old ladies sitting by the window. I remember one had a walker—"

"Think of some people who might actually have a crush on you!" Solana clarified.

"Well, it didn't seem like anyone did. There was a group of guys from my English class sitting at the big table over there."

"Who specifically?" asked Tyler.

"Josiah and some others. I don't know. I've hardly talked to any of them."

Jacie swiveled toward Hannah. "Do you think it was the secret admirer?"

"Are you getting more visits from our anonymous friend?" Dinah asked. Hannah had kept her aunt informed since the gifts started arriving almost a year ago. It seemed every few months—just when Hannah would forget about the mysterious admirer—he'd show up again.

"She got a very sweet note in her locker this morning," Jacie volunteered.

"I'm telling you. If you want him to go away, you should act interested in him," Solana said.

"How can I act interested in someone when I don't know who it is?"

Solana shrugged. "We'll think of something. But acting

interested will scare him away. The theory works. Kassidy pours out all her attention on Galvin, and he doesn't give her the time of day. I ignore him completely, and he tries to start up a conversation with me."

"So you're saying Hannah should become a flirt in order to keep guys away from her?" asked Becca.

"Exactly. And I can give her lessons."

"No, thanks," Hannah said.

"Oh, it's so easy. You just ask a few questions, bat your eyes, smile big . . . then they'll think, 'Hmmm, she's not as intriguing as I thought. She's just a flirty girl like everyone else.' They'll fly out of there before you can say . . . well . . . something really short."

"Jell-O pop!" Jacie suggested.

Solana rolled her eyes. "Uh . . . sure."

Hannah didn't say anything. She believed in not dating until you found "the one," but it was becoming increasingly more complicated to avoid guys altogether. Tyler had come along as a package deal with her circle of friends and, except for the first few months, it hadn't been awkward. But other guys made her nervous and irritated, even when she was attracted to them, which she rarely admitted, even to herself. Fortunately, except for this mysterious admirer, things seemed pretty clear. No romantic entanglements.

Becca had a boyfriend, Nate. Jacie occasionally hung out with Damien, but just as friends. Tyler was usually in the middle of some awkward crush. And Solana, of course, was dealing with her own relational dilemma—even if she was choosing to ignore it for the time being. *But me . . . I'm in the free and clear. No relational stresses.* Even so, she kind of envied them. She no longer doubted that courtship was right for her. But she really wondered quite often, more than she'd ever let her friends know, *Who is this secret admirer?* Whoever he was, he brought her warm thoughts and feelings. Lying in her attic she'd read his notes over and over, imagining what he could look like. Who he was. Sometimes she'd fall asleep seeing herself walking toward a tall, handsome man. *Someday*, she would say, holding the feelings close to her. *Someday*.

c h a p t e r 4

Hannah was lost in thought as she mindlessly spun her locker combination. How *was* God using her now? Maybe she was missing something. Maybe God was telling her something but she wasn't hearing Him. He couldn't possibly just want to "grow her character" as her aunt suggested. He always had a purpose for people. Of that she was sure. She'd have to ask Dinah on Sunday.

"Hi, Hannah." A male voice behind her rang above the hallway chatter and her own unanswered questions.

Hannah automatically turned around. *Galvin.*

"Hi—" She said tentatively. She had to agree with Solana. Galvin was good-looking. Chiseled features, a strong jaw, dark hair, tanned face, nice smile. But what should she say to him? Was he going to try to get on her good side in hopes that she would get him an "in" with Solana? She wouldn't be used so easily. "Do I know you?"

"I'm Galvin Parker." He stuck out his hand to shake hers. *Strong grip*, Hannah noticed. Not many high school guys shook hands, and she liked that he did. "I just started here this year. I sit a few rows behind you in chemistry."

Hannah nodded. She hadn't noticed. But she couldn't say that. She forced a polite smile. "Welcome to Stony Brook." *Maybe that's it, maybe he won't ask me anything else. I don't want to get in the middle of Sol's experiment.* She turned around.

"Wait!" Galvin called.

Shoot.

"I mean, I wanted to talk to you about something."

Couldn't he see all the curious expressions of people going by? Couldn't he tell she wasn't comfortable having a conversation with him in the middle of a busy hallway?

"What?"

"I thought . . . maybe . . ."

Just spit it out. If you want Solana's number . . .

". . . could we be lab partners?"

The smile. She recognized that smile. She hadn't always, but in the past year she'd grown more accustomed to it and knew what it meant. *He likes me. Oh, shoot, he likes me.* This wasn't supposed to happen. Now what? Solana's words from yesterday flew to mind: *You just ask a few questions, bat your eyes, smile big . . . they'll fly out of there before—*

Hannah took a deep breath. Solana seemed to know what she was talking about. *Okay . . . let's see how this works.*

Galvin shifted impatiently. "What do you think?"

"Sure," she smiled.

"Really?" He looked like he was about to fall over.

"Why not?" she said, her mind racing. *Ask questions. What am I supposed to ask him? Why did the chicken cross the road? Are you Calvinist or Arminian? Are you on any mind-altering medication?* "How are you at chemistry?"

"I'm pretty good. I got a hundred on our first exam."

"Good. Do you play sports?" She batted her eyes, feeling very stupid. *Girls actually did this?* It gave her a headache.

"Basketball . . . and a little bit of baseball. But basketball is more my thing." He paused. "Do you have something in your eye?"

She stopped batting. "Um . . . not anymore."

"Cool. I'm really excited about being lab partners. I mean, the other guys were saying that—um, I'm just glad you agreed."

Wait a minute. Wasn't he supposed to be running the other way by now? "You still want to be lab partners?"

"Of course. Why else would I ask you?"

"But I *really* want to be lab partners. I mean, you'd probably be my favorite lab partner in the whole class." *There you go, Hannah. Pour it on thick.*

"Wow. I'm flattered. Y'know, if you're not doing anything next weekend maybe we could go out. Let's talk about it in class. I need to run."

And he was off, whistling and doing a little jig thing with his feet.

That didn't work very well.

She clapped her hand over her mouth. *Was* HE *her secret admirer? He couldn't be, could he? He just started school here.* Hannah sighed. Whatever, she'd just blown it big time.

Stupidity: *Following Soluna's advice on dealing with boys.*

● ● ●

"How are the layouts looking, Hannah?" Mr. Collins asked.

"Pretty good." She stepped back so the faculty advisor for the school newspaper could see her progress on this week's sports page. "I'm not really much of a sports person, to be honest with you."

"You might want to go with this shot instead," he said, pointing to a photo on the computer monitor. "More action."

Hannah nodded in agreement. "And the portrait orientation will balance the page better."

Mr. Collins looked closer at the screen, examining the photos Hannah had taken with the digital camera. "You've got such a great eye, even if you're not into sports."

"Thanks." Hannah had always liked the gray-haired teacher. He was straight-laced, but always warm. And he didn't sugarcoat things, so his compliments were genuine—not just meant to boost a kid's self-esteem.

"Which brings me to a question I have for you." Mr. Collins stood upright, his arms folded.

"Yes?"

"As you know, next week is homecoming, meaning we have a big paper to get out on Friday." The newspaper staff had to have the paper completed on Thursday at four in order to get it printed in time for distribution on Friday morning.

"We'll all work really hard this week, Mr. Collins."

"I know you will. Especially you."

"Sir?"

"Because I would like you to design the central photo spread."

Hannah's mouth dropped. "Really?" Traditionally, at the center of the extra-large issue was a two-page photo layout, a collage of photos from homecoming events. But usually the editor and assistant editor designed major layouts like that—not the staff photographer.

"What about—"

"I think you've got a better eye for it. And you'll be more familiar with the photos you have in stock. Besides, Brendan and Alicia will be swamped."

Hannah felt her cheeks redden. She felt flattered, but what

if she let Mr. Collins down? Although she carried a decent amount of confidence in her photography and Photoshop skills, she didn't have a lot of experience with design. What if she let the newspaper staff down? What if she let the school down? What if *everyone* was really disappointed? *Could you believe that stupid photo layout? It ruined the entire issue. And it's usually so good. Must've been that new photographer. What an embarrassment to Stony Brook!*

"Hannah?"

"Oh, sorry." Hannah shook out the thoughts.

"Maybe I shouldn't have assumed you'd be interested. I realize it will take some extra time."

"No, no. I want to do it."

Mr. Collins grinned. "Great. I know you'll do an impressive job. It's always the highlight of the homecoming issue."

No pressure. But even while her stomach did nervous flips, a euphoric high flooded into her bloodstream. *Mr. Collins thinks I'm talented. He gave me the best part of the paper! The heading will read "HOMECOMING! Photos and design by Hannah Connor."* The thought was almost enough to make her forget the disastrous conversation with Galvin Parker. Almost.

● ● ●

Dr. Hanson tapped on his assignment sheet and pushed his glasses up his nose. He was the only teacher Hannah had ever seen who wore blue-rimmed glasses. She wondered if they were his midlife crisis buy. Since he couldn't afford a BMW convertible or hair implants, he got wild blue-rimmed glasses. He was the kind of person who always seemed awkward and nervous, making everyone around him feel awkward and nervous, too.

The chemistry instructor cleared his throat and tapped faster. "Since we're done with our first section, we're now ready to start experimenting with a lab partner. Well, not really *with* a lab partner. I don't mean performing experiments on a lab partner. Not at all. I mean . . . in conjunction with a lab partner. So you and your lab partner will experiment together on something completely different than each other."

The class stared blankly.

"And, in fact, I think we already covered this yesterday. Because today we were going to choose partners. I'm giving you the option of choosing a lab partner, and for those who choose not to choose, I'll match up those of you who choose to be left." He blinked. "That's a lot of *chooses*, isn't it? So, who's made a choi—a decision?"

Murmurings began as people who'd forgotten to get paired up beforehand turned in their seats to find a partner. Several others raised their hands.

"Yes, Monica?"

"Alyssa and I are partnering together."

"Very good. And Kassidy?"

"I'll be partnering with Galvin. If that's okay with you, Galvin."

Hannah watched Galvin out of the corner of her eye. Maybe he'd forgotten the earlier conversation. Maybe he'd realized that Hannah was far too interested in him for him to be comfortable as her lab partner. Maybe he would prefer to be Kassidy's partner and now that the opportunity had arisen, he'd jump at the chance.

"Actually, Hannah and I decided to be partners."

The murmuring in the class went silent. Kassidy's face turned deep red, and Hannah felt the fire being sent in her direction. Dr. Hanson even seemed surprised.

"Hannah Connor?"

I'm the only Hannah in the class.

"Yes, Hannah Connor," Galvin repeated.

"Okay." Dr. Hanson pushed his glasses up again as he rummaged through his planning book. "Hannah Connor and Galvin Parker."

Well, let's just say it again, everyone! Hannah Connor and Galvin Parker are lab partners. Announce it over the PA system. Maybe someone hasn't heard yet.

Hannah clasped her hands together on her desk, trying to act normal—as though it were just like her to team up with the best-looking boy in class.

Other students chose their partners. Dr. Hanson explained the two-day experiment that would start Monday. And the entire time, Hannah felt the eyes of Kassidy Jordan boring through her.

chapter 5

Jacie threw her hands in the air. "Can you believe it? What am I going to do?!"

Solana shook her head. "I don't even know why you're surprised. Everyone knows you're one of the most well-liked girls at school."

Hannah nodded in agreement. Her three closest friends lounged around her impeccably neat room—Solana across the bed, Becca in the big wicker chair, and Jacie cross-legged on the floor. Those were pretty much the only places to sit in her small attic room. Except the gray-shingled roof outside her window—her personal favorite spot.

"We all expected it," said Becca.

It was true. When the homecoming court candidates were announced at the end of the day, no one had been surprised when Jacie's name was announced. No one except Jacie, that is. But she seemed like a natural choice. With her easy spark of a smile and genuine concern for other people, she was friends with the entire senior class.

"But think about last year's homecoming queen!" said Jacie.

"Ming Jasmine? What about her?" Becca asked.

"She was perfect! She was gorgeous and athletic and fun and brilliant. Ming Jasmines are the kind of people who are supposed to be homecoming queens! Not Jacie Nolands!" argued Jacie.

"Well, this year it's going to be Jacie Noland. Jessica Abbott and Kassidy Jordan don't stand a chance," Solana said.

Hannah hoped Solana was right. None of the girls were particularly fond of Jessica—who flirted with Tyler unmercifully. And, after today's chemistry experience, she wasn't a Kassidy Jordan fan either.

"You could at least be excited about it," added Becca. "Most girls would consider this an honor—not the ruination of their lives."

"Well, other girls don't have the same concerns I do," said Jacie. "I was planning on wearing the same dress I wore to the homecoming dance last year, but if I'm in the court, I'll need to get something more formal."

Speaking of clothes, I should probably change into what I'm wearing tonight, since that's why we stopped by the house anyway, Hannah thought. She got up to sort through her small freestanding wardrobe closet.

"True," said Solana.

"But that costs money. Money that I don't have. And money I don't want to ask my mom for."

Jacie's mom and dad had never married, and so Ms. Noland had raised her daughter by herself the last 17 years. She was a woman much like Jacie, fun and sweet, the girls all liked her. But she needed to work long hours to provide for the two of them, and a new formal dress certainly wouldn't be in the budget.

Hannah fumbled through a multitude of blouses. "Maybe you could borrow something." She caught sight of the slinky black dress she'd picked up at a thrift store a couple of years ago and thought about showing it to Jacie. *No, that's my secret.* Besides, what would her friends think of her if they knew she kind of liked things like that? They thought of her as such a strong Christian.

"Yeah, like anything any of you three own would fit me." Jacie folded her arms in discouragement. "And the other thing is that traditionally, the girls' fathers escort them down the field at halftime. Good chance of that happening with my dad."

Bennett Crosse lived outside of San Francisco. Although he loved his daughter and enjoyed having her come visit a couple of times a year, he never really filled the "dad role" in Jacie's life. *But maybe this time he would,* thought Hannah.

"You could always call and ask him. He'd probably love to escort you, and he'd only have to fly in for a day," Hannah said.

"It's true, Jacie. There's no harm in checking," said Becca.

Jacie shrugged. "It just seems like a lot to ask. I mean, this is a big deal for me, but Dad's kind of beyond high school culture." Jacie paused for a minute. "Maybe I will call him—just to see."

"How can it take you so long to find something to wear, Hannah?" complained Solana, glancing up from her magazine. "With your wardrobe, you either choose 'super-conservative' or 'ultra-conservative.' Be daring, go with super."

"I think super-conservative would be more daring for *you*," Hannah responded. Solana wore tight black jeans and a lime green top exposing her midriff. And that was about as "conservative" as she'd ever seen the girl.

"We are not going to have another clothes debate," insisted Becca. She'd been toying with Hannah's Rubik's Cube. "But please hurry, it's sweltering up here."

That was true. Hannah could feel the warm dampness soaking through her shirt. This time of year, Colorado weather changed as often as Solana did. Yesterday's freezing winds melted into today's heat wave. "Sorry about that." She didn't know why it took so long for her to decide. They were just going to meet Tyler and Nate for movies at Becca's house. She pulled out a pink T-shirt and a long denim skirt.

"We'll go shopping with you tomorrow morning, Jacie," Solana suggested. "There has to be something out there that would be affordable."

"That would be great. Would you mind?" Jacie bit her lip.

"It'll be fun," said Becca. "Are you in, Hannah?"

"I'll run it past my parents, but it should be fine." She hurriedly ran a brush through her long, blonde hair, happy that her parents were allowing her more freedom than they used to. It still wasn't close to the liberty her friends enjoyed, but it was more than she'd had in the past. The fact that Mr. and Mrs. Connor were protective hadn't bothered her when she was home-schooled. But since she'd started attending Stony Brook last year, she realized that many of her friends' parents granted more autonomy than hers did. Sometimes it made her feel incredibly loved that her parents were so concerned about her well-being, and sometimes, well—frankly, it could be annoying, although she'd never dare speak that way about her parents.

"I don't know why you had to change in the first place," said Solana. "Taking off a skirt to put on another doesn't seem like much of a change to me."

Hannah slipped on her leather loafers.

"You're not trying to impress Nate, are you?" teased Becca.

"You'd put me in the hospital," Hannah teased back. Becca and Nate had been dating for almost six months, and Becca still got giddy about him.

"Okay, I'm ready."

"Becca, I don't think you'll have to worry about Hannah," said Jacie, joining the other girls as they retreated downstairs.

"Unless her whole courtship commitment is only a farce so we don't see her coming after our men," laughed Solana.

"Like our favorite Barbie doll would have any competition." Jacie's words were said under the pounding of steps down the attic stairs, but Hannah still heard them.

Her cheeks flushed, but she felt secretly pleased. The girls often bemoaned that Hannah's perfect figure and flawless face were wasted underneath her conventional wardrobe, and she usually responded embarrassed and uncomfortable. But, tonight, she felt like looking nice. *No reason. I just feel like looking nice.*

● ● ●

"La-de-dah-de-dah. Guess who decided to come home." Tyler was getting out of his car as the girls pulled into the driveway. Nate leaned against the passenger door.

"You just got here yourself." Solana extricated herself from the backseat.

"We were expecting you to have the home-baked snacks all ready by now," teased Nate, giving a wink to Becca.

"Yeah, right," Becca said. She'd said herself that she could cook about as well as a weasel.

Hannah noticed Tyler had half a Milky Way in hand. "You couldn't have had too much faith if you stopped to get a snack for the road."

"Merely an appetizer." He chomped off a bite of nougat.

"Plus it was a God-ordained pit stop according to Tyler," said Nate.

"Must be a good candy bar," said Becca.

"I was just telling Nate that it feels like God is already preparing me for CU Boulder," Tyler said. "It seems like every day I'm meeting another person who goes there and loves it. Today, I met this chick . . ."

Four dirty looks turned his way.

"I mean babe . . ."

Four dirtier looks continued to stare.

"I mean *girl* in the grocery store. When I ran in for the Milky Way. She was in front of me in line wearing a CU-B T-shirt. I told her I would be starting there next fall. She's a sophomore, home for the weekend."

"Man, you can pick up women anywhere," Nate said. "Did you get her number?"

"C'mon, I'm going to be a lowly freshman when she's a junior," he said before muttering under his breath, "although she *did* give me her name and told me to look her up next year."

"You're pathetic," Solana said.

"I'm just ready to get out of the house," Tyler muttered. "Today reminded me of that."

No one had to ask him to expound. They knew about Tyler's volatile dad.

"Don't ask me about it yet. Just feed me and let me kick some rear in Trivial Pursuit."

● ● ●

"Sweden," Becca said. "I think it's Sweden."

"What about Ireland?" asked Nate. "That's pretty far north."

"I'm not even sure that's a Scandinavian country," said Solana. "I should have paid more attention in geography class."

"I thought you loved geography class," said Becca.

"I loved the looks of Mr. Hankins who taught geography class, but the whole countries and maps and stuff really bored me," Solana explained.

"Your time is almost up, Team Two," said Tyler. "I'll repeat the question. What's the northernmost Scandinavian country?"

"Is Scandinavia a country?" asked Becca.

"I think so," said Nate.

"Let's go with that. Scandinavia is our answer," said Solana.

"Bzzzz." Tyler took great joy in being a human buzzer. "Wrong answer."

"Was it Sweden?" asked Hannah.

"Nope. Norway."

"Norway is a country?" said Nate.

"Yeah. My dad's ancestors are from there," said Tyler as he tossed the die across the board.

"So what happened with your dad tonight?" Jacie cautiously broached the subject.

Tyler shrugged, as though letting the memory roll off his shoulders. "The typical. I come home from school, grab a snack, and I'm about ready to go out to get the mail. I saw Dad's car in the driveway and knew that he was home, but figured he took an early flight and was sleeping. So he comes into the kitchen and lays into me about leaving my backpack on the kitchen counter. I mean, a simple 'Could you put your backpack away?' would have sufficed, but you'd have thought I was storing dead bodies in the freezer the way he went off on me."

"Let me guess," said Solana. "You argued back."

"You know me. I try, I really do try, to make peace with him." Tyler's hands shook as he played with the trivia card in his hand. "But I told him I'd take care of it and he could calm down."

"Uh, oh." Hannah had only met Mr. Jennings a handful of times, but she knew Tyler's reaction wouldn't go over well.

"And he told me he'd calm down when I started doing my share around the house, and, well, you know the whole deal," Tyler said.

"So what did you do then?" asked Nate.

"I stood there until he was done lecturing me. Then I grabbed my backpack, and took off on my bike. I hung out at the library and IM'd Allen until I came here."

Hannah was glad Tyler had the sense to IM his former youth pastor. They'd continued a mentoring relationship even after Allen moved away a couple of years ago, and the older man often gave Tyler wise advice.

Jacie laid a gentle hand on Tyler's arm. "I'm sorry."

"I know. Me, too. But I think I'm kind of used to it now."

"Going away to school will definitely be good for you," said Solana. She picked up a trivia card. "Your team's turn, Tyler."

Tyler, Jacie, and Hannah perked up.

Solana cleared her throat before reading the next Trivial Pursuit question. "What card is removed from the deck in Old Maid?"

"Old Maid! I've never played Old Maid!" said Tyler.

"You have too," said Jacie. "We all played when we were kids."

"But not with a regular deck," Becca said. "They have that funky deck."

"A queen," Hannah said. "One of the queens is removed."

"Which one?" asked Tyler.

"It doesn't matter. Just one of them," answered Hannah.

"She's right! Queen of the Old Maids. Congratulations, Hannah."

"I can't believe you knew that," Tyler said.

"When you have a big family and not a lot of money, you learn a lot of card games." The truth was, Hannah enjoyed breaking out a deck of cards with her family. And Old Maid could be kind of fun.

Jacie rolled the die and moved to a yellow spot.

"I'll read this question," said Becca, picking a card. "What philosopher was hailed by Hitler and Mussolini as the prophet of authoritarianism?"

Hannah, Tyler, and Jacie looked at each other with blank expressions.

"Uh, Plato?" Tyler ventured.

"Friedrich Nietzsche. Our turn."

Nate rolled the die. "Science. It's all yours, Solana."

Hannah picked a card. "What's the better-known identity of minus 273.15 degrees Celsius?"

"Don't insult me," Solana said. "It's absolute zero."

"She's right."

"Oh," Tyler said. "I thought absolute zero was the progress you were making with Galvin Parker."

Hannah's heart did a funny flip at the name.

"Very funny." Solana added a green piece to their pie. "For your information things between Galvin and me are progressing very well. He smiled at me again today."

Hannah tried to think of a way to change the subject. She didn't want to talk about Galvin. What if someone told Solana that she and Galvin were pairing up for the chemistry assignment? Then she'd have to explain that Galvin might kinda-sorta like her.

"This has to be killing you, going so slow," said Becca.

"To be honest, I think I need the time. I'm still thinking of Ramón a lot."

Hannah knew Solana must be hurting pretty deeply for her to share something like that. She hadn't wanted to share her conversation with Galvin earlier for that very reason. If Galvin gave Solana a reason to get over Ramón, she wanted to help her do it. *Granted, I'd rather see her let God help her get over Ramón.* But that certainly wasn't looking too likely. If Solana knew Galvin had an interest in Hannah, she'd be even more discouraged and depressed. *No, it's best this way. Besides, Galvin will tire of me in no time. I'll make sure of it.*

It didn't take long for Solana, Becca, and Nate to win the game. Among the three of them, any question having to do with science, entertainment, and sports was covered.

"Pizza's here!" Mrs. McKinnon called from upstairs.

Hannah laughed as the gang of friends thumped passed her in their hurry to get up the stairs. The warm smells of pepperoni and cheese made her stomach growl, and she followed close behind.

Hannah marveled at how comfortable she felt in the McKinnon home. The group had hung out here every Friday night for over a year. Well, actually for several years before then, but she hadn't been a part of them until she joined Stony Brook at the beginning of her junior year. Becca's parents had the perfect place for kids to hang out—foosball, large screen TV, Ping-Pong table, and plenty of food. The group had been here almost every day this past summer—playing around in the McKinnons' pool and having flip competitions on their giant trampoline.

"So, what's the movie tonight?" asked Solana, between mouthfuls of pizza.

"We've got a couple choices," Becca said, grabbing a stack of DVDs off the kitchen table and handing them to Solana.

These were true friends, Hannah thought. People who loved you even when you blew it on a missions trip. People who would stand by you even if the guy you loved left town or you didn't have the money for a homecoming dress. People who knew each other inside out and loved each other anyway.

Tyler grabbed for a breadstick. "I was thinking we could do a Monopoly tournament."

"No way," said Nate. "You're no fun to play with."

"Can I help it if I'm a king in real estate?"

"A king who talks with his mouth full," said Becca, Solana, and Hannah in unison.

Comfort: *When five contradicting personalities blend even better than cheese and pepperoni.*

chapter 6

Hannah opened her curtains to a bright, sunny Saturday—a perfect day for dress shopping. She padded downstairs in her bathrobe. Eating Fruity Pebbles while watching cartoons with the little ones had become a Saturday morning tradition.

"It's about time you got up!" said Elijah, already curled up in his spot on the couch.

The clock in the kitchen read 7:04. *Hardly late*. Hannah poured the sugary cereal into three bowls and drowned them in milk.

The morning passed through *Captain Caveman*, *Recess*, and a *VeggieTales* video. Mr. and Mrs. Connor came down around 8:30, dressed in sweats to clean out the garage.

"I'm so glad you take care of them on Saturdays," her mom said, giving Hannah a kiss on the cheek.

"No problem." Hannah would never admit she looked forward to Saturday morning cartoon time with five-year-olds.

She ran the shopping plans past her parents, and reminded them about going to The Edge that evening. The conglomeration of youth groups from area churches met for a big rally and game time one Saturday a month.

"Sounds like we won't be seeing you much today," her dad said.

"I guess not." Hannah loved that her parents were big into family time, but she hoped they wouldn't ask her to stay home tonight. "But I should be around all day tomorrow."

"That would be wonderful," said Mrs. Connor. "I could use your help getting ready for Dinah and Greg."

"That's right!" Hannah had forgotten her aunt's promise to come over for dinner before they left for Kenya.

Mrs. Connor spoke in a hushed voice so the twins wouldn't hear. Not that it was likely—the two were enthralled with the French Peas singing on-screen. "Dinah is telling the other kids about the baby being a G-I-R-L."

The baby! Hannah instantly knew what she wanted to do: She'd throw Dinah a shower when she got back from Africa. Jacie, Solana, and Becca would love to help—she was sure. It would be so much fun, she couldn't wait to tell them.

● ● ●

"What do you think about having the shower colors yellow and white?" Hannah asked over the table of two Cokes, one carrot juice, and one mocha malt Frappuccino.

"Why are we planning this already, Hannah? The shower won't be for a couple months," said Solana.

"I'm so excited about it. And I know the women at her church will throw her one closer to her due date. I want to give her the first one." Hannah sat with her pen poised over a steno pad, waiting for the great ideas to flow.

"Maybe a soft pink," suggested Jacie.

"Gag. Why don't they ever decorate baby showers in red? Or silver?" asked Solana.

"Sure. If it's going to be a disco baby," laughed Becca.

Jacie struck a John Travolta pose. "What a great theme. We could have a disco ball . . ."

"And wear sequins . . ." added Solana.

"This is a baby shower. Not Halloween," Hannah said.

Solana crossed her hands over her chest. "You always go by the rules."

What was so wrong about going by the rules? She imagined Dinah walking into a dark room with a disco ball spinning from the ceiling, and everyone dressed in sequined tube tops and sporting feathered hair.

"No disco shower," Hannah said.

"Your aunt would think it was cool," said Becca, sipping her carrot juice.

True. Aunt Dinah loved the unexpected. *She'd* certainly never been accused of going by the rules too much.

"But my mom will be there. And . . ."

"It's not like we'd have to wear sequined tube tops."

Hannah changed the picture in her mind to the woman sitting around with feather boas and ruffled blouses. But still . . .

"Yellow ducks," she said firmly, making a note of it.

Solana rolled her eyes. "Oh, goody."

Becca pulled her date book out of her purse. "We'll have to set up an organizational meeting in the next couple of weeks."

Hannah loved that Becca was such a planner. If anyone got things done, it was her.

"What about next Saturday?" asked Jacie.

"Can't," said Becca. "I promised the kids at the Community Center we'd go hiking." She scanned through a few pages. "With all the homecoming stuff next week, I think we'll need to plan it for the week after."

"Let's worry about that later, then," said Solana. She slurped up the last bit of her Frappuccino with a gurgling noise. "We need to get shopping."

"Yeah, I need to be at work by one." Jacie worked at Raggs by Razz, a popular clothing store that catered to teens.

Hannah had somewhat prided herself in not going along with the crowd. But she'd noticed lately that the girls had talked her into buying a piece here and there that was a bit more fashionable. A belt, some clunky shoes, a purse, cargo pants, and, well, she kind of liked them.

"So where do we start?" asked Becca.

Jacie pulled out a list of some of the department stores and discount clothing shops she favored. "Remember, though, look for clearance!"

The four girls made their way to a nearby department store. "I left my dad a message about flying out for homecoming and told him I'd call him back tonight," Jacie said.

"Do you think he'll come?" asked Hannah.

Jacie shrugged. "It's not like he doesn't have the money to fly out, but I'm not sure he'll be able to take the time."

Hannah had never met Jacie's dad, but she knew he was a successful art curator who served as a board member for a number of charities. It was easy to see where Jacie got her artistic abilities and her compassion for people. Unfortunately, Mr. Crosse's compassion was so taken up by his volunteer work, he didn't have much left for his daughter.

"You know my dad," Jacie said. "Of course, he'd love to come, but chances are he'll have some fund-raising event or gallery opening or something."

"Who will you have escort you if he can't make it?" asked Solana.

"I haven't thought that far ahead yet."

Six stores later, nothing had caught Jacie's eye.

"How about this?" asked Hannah, reaching for a yellow slim-cut, floor-length dress with cap sleeves.

Jacie shook her head. "Not my style."

"Too boring is what you mean," said Solana. "*This* is what you're after." She held up a tight black silk dress, with lots of crisscrossing straps around the front and back. "Pretty hot, huh?"

"I think I'd strangle myself trying to get it over my head." Jacie continued to thumb through a clearance rack. "What am I going to do? There's nothing here!"

Becca picked up Hannah's arm to look at her watch. "And you need to be at work in 20 minutes."

Jacie sighed her disappointment at not having found a dress. "I don't know where else to look. Let's go grab some lunch."

"Great, I'm starved." Solana put back the dress and led the group out of the store toward the food court. "You're being really picky though, Jace. We found some cute dresses today."

"I know, and I appreciate you all helping me. But the dresses, well, they just weren't what I had in mind."

"So maybe it would help to know what you have in mind," Becca suggested.

Jacie shook her head. "I fell in love with a dress in the window at Raggs."

"Perfect. Don't you get an employee's discount?" asked Hannah.

"Except on in-season formal wear. After homecoming I'll get a discount, but that's a little too late," Jacie said. "Besides, this dress would be too expensive even with my discount."

"Yikes, that must be pricey," Becca said.

The four headed to the line at Chick-fil-A.

"Yeah, you'll never believe who else was looking at it earlier this week," Jacie said.

"Who?" asked Solana.

"Your favorite Galvin-competitor."

"Kassidy Jordan?!" Solana asked.

Hannah swallowed.

"Yep, but it was too pricey for her, too. By the way, Hannah, have you ever talked to her?"

Hannah still hadn't told the girls about her interactions with Galvin. But how could she explain why Kassidy disliked her without bringing it up?

"She's in my chemistry class. Why do you ask?"

"Well, it sounded like she was talking about you with her friend while they were in the store."

"I don't think she likes me very much. I got paired up with Galvin for an experiment we're doing Monday and Tuesday, and she was hoping for the spot," said Hannah.

"You didn't tell me you were doing chemistry with Galvin!" squealed Solana. "Just make sure the sparks stay on the Bunsen burner."

"Like you have to worry with Hannah," said Becca. "You're better off with her as his partner than anyone." She stepped up to order her lunch.

"Hannah, now you'll have a chance to say a few things about me. Kind of mysterious, but positive, like—" Solana began.

"Oh, no," said Hannah. "Don't include me in my experiment."

After the girls received their supply of chicken nuggets and waffle fries, they crowded around a too-small food court table.

Hannah usually didn't care what people thought of her, but curiosity was getting the best of her.

"So what did Kassidy say about me?"

"Not much. It was actually kind of funny. She said something about your 'prissy façade' being a cover-up for being a 'man-eater.'"

Solana snorted while taking a sip of her Coke, and she began coughing and laughing at the same time. "Man-eater?" she gasped between coughs.

"I wonder why she would say that?" Becca said, pounding Solana's back until the coughs subsided.

"Hey! Enough already," Solana said, whacking Becca's arm away.

"Sor-ry," Becca said. "I was only trying to help."

"I probably shouldn't even say this, but she also referred to you as 'Hannah the Hypocrite,'" Jacie said through a mouthful of fries. "She must've really wanted to be Galvin's lab partner."

"I think she wants to be more than lab partners," Solana said. "And Kassidy usually gets what she wants. She'd start these horrible rumors about me in middle school whenever I was after the same guy she was, just to keep him away from me. It got pretty messy."

Becca nodded. "And she's still getting what she wants. She's the most stuck-up girl in our class and she's on the homecoming court."

"Some people can be so blind," said Solana. "Why can't the nerds and geeks realize that she only becomes friendly with them two weeks before homecoming court election?"

"I hope she doesn't start any rumors about you," Jacie said to Hannah.

Solana shrugged. "What could she possibly say about Hannah that anyone would believe? She's like the Blonde Angel of Copper Ridge. They'll hand everyone else a diploma and make Hannah a saint."

"I'm not that . . ." Hannah searched for a word. ". . . sain-tish," she said. Sure, she dressed and acted more conservatively than most girls her age, but she was just like them, right? A lack of flashy clothes didn't make her personality boring.

"I'm just saying there's not much Kassidy can do to ruin

your reputation. You're as squeaky clean as one of those dish-washing commercials," Solana said. "You're a shoo-in to become a pastor's wife."

Hannah concentrated on her nuggets. She knew Solana meant her words to be comforting, but why did they bother her so much?

● ● ●

Pound, pound, pound, pound.

Hannah's feet hit the pavement as she ran through her neighborhood. She couldn't get away from the words. They chanted along with the rhythm of her feet.

Hannah the hypocrite. Hannah the hypocrite.

Why did she care so much what Kassidy thought of her?

Pound, pound, pound.

Kassidy doesn't even know me. I should be thinking about more important things. She thought about the stack of college applications on her small desk at home.

Pound, pound, pound.

Like school . . . and a major.

When she was little she'd wanted to be a veterinarian. Her pet hamster Sparky got his foot stuck in his wheel and sprained it, so Hannah made him a cast out of duct tape. When her mom saw, she made Hannah take it off. Hannah never heard a hamster squeal like Sparky did that day. The poor hamster died a week later.

Then she'd wanted to be a teacher. She'd sat her little brothers and sisters down to teach them how to read. But it only ended in an argument when Micah said he'd eat green eggs and ham if someone gave him the chance, but he only got peanut butter. Rebekah hopped onto the complainer train because she had to eat a plain white bologna sandwich—which she promptly refused. Daniel hid his sandwich under the couch, and Mrs. Connor didn't find it until two weeks later. And the twins just cried. She still helped her little brothers and sisters with their schoolwork, but teaching never seemed quite as appealing after that.

She always thought she'd be a wife, a mom, even home-school like her own family. *There's nothing wrong with that. But I need to go to school for something.*

Math? *I'd die of boredom.* Photography? *Could I take that as a major?* English? *Maybe . . . but what would I do with it?* Biblical studies? *Reverend Hannah . . . probably not.*

Go to librarian school. You've got the wardrobe for it, she could almost hear Solana's voice. Or was that Kassidy's? Somehow it was more okay for Solana to make fun of her, because at least she knew, despite their differences, Solana genuinely respected and cared for Hannah. And vice versa. But Kassidy didn't.

Hannah pushed herself to speed up as she passed Pine Grove Park. A blanket of fallen leaves covered the sidewalk and crunched under her feet like potato chips. She loved running in this kind of weather. The air smelled fresh and free.

A shriek of laughter interrupted her thoughts.

The tight-jean clan circled around a couple baseball play-ers who'd just finished their game. Cozy, fuchsia-lipped smiles moved a mile a minute—deep into some conversation. *They won't even notice me*, Hannah thought.

No such luck.

"Well, Hannah," Kassidy's high-pitched squeal reeked with sarcasm. "You're not wearing a skirt. Aren't you afraid you'll go to hell?"

Her friends, Courtney and Cherise, giggled next to her.

Hannah felt her tongue balloon up like an enormous lump of bread dough. Should she answer with some witty-yet-Christian response or should she ignore the girl? No witty-yet-Christian response came to mind, so she chose the latter. She jogged past—within a couple feet of the group, willing her feet to move faster.

"Better be careful," called Cherise. "Your bloomers are showing."

Annoyance: *People who think they're saying something funny and original when you've already heard it a hundred times.*

A crowd of little kids playing hopscotch on the sidewalk forced her to slow her pace. She had no choice but to stop.

"Hi, girls," she tried to smile. "Bloomers aren't very good for running."

The baseball players watched curiously. Hannah felt her heart pounding in her chest—but it wasn't from running.

Kassidy narrowed her eyes. "You're changing in so many ways. First you become a flirt and then you change your dress. Maybe this will impress Galvin, hmm?"

"I'm not interested in impressing Galvin," Hannah said. Her mind flashed back to her faux-flirtatious hallway conversation. *Please, God, make sure no one overheard that.*

"You could've fooled me. I'm thinking we should change your nickname from Holy Hannah to Hypocritical Hannah," Kassidy said.

Hannah felt her face redden and a lump rise in her throat. How dare this girl who didn't even know her talk to her that way. She'd never done anything to Kassidy. Hannah bit her tongue. She wanted to argue back. *Galvin doesn't like you, and who could blame him?* She wanted to spit the words in her face. But she knew it was wrong, and the look on Kassidy's face hinted that it wouldn't be forgotten either.

"I need to go," she said, and she turned to resume her run.

Pound, pound, pound.

Kassidy's catty words followed her. "Just watch out, Miss Priss."

Hannah kept going, refusing to look back.

● ● ●

Ding-dong. The Connor doorbell echoed throughout the house and Hannah was opening the door before the sound finished resonating. The kitchen clock read 7:20. Her friends were already late.

"Hi, we need to stop by Tyler's house before we go to The Edge." Becca's words came out in a rush.

"What's going on?" Hannah asked as she hurried to the car.

"Tyler got his letter from CU Boulder. We need to go celebrate."

"He got in?"

"We think so. They're sending out acceptance letters this week and Tyler's mom just called to tell him he got an envelope from them."

The only person who hadn't seemed to catch the electricity in the car was Jacie. She silently stared out the car window.

"Are you okay?" Hannah asked her, while the rest of the group sang along to a Beach Boys song.

Jacie shrugged. "I shouldn't be surprised."

"About Tyler?"

"I called my dad earlier today about coming out for homecoming—"

"And . . ." But Hannah already knew the answer.

"He can't come. Which, of course, I knew was a long shot anyway. I don't know why I even got my hopes up."

Hannah didn't know what to say, except, "I'm sorry."

"It's not a big deal. Really. Like I said, I knew it would happen this way." She stared out the window. "I just wish it could be . . . different."

● ● ●

The CD player shut off abruptly.

"C'mon, let's go," Tyler said, already halfway out of the car.

Tyler sprinted up the driveway and into his house, with the girls close behind. Hannah wondered if Mr. Jennings was home.

Mrs. Jennings, an editor of *Brio* magazine, greeted the rest of the kids. "You certainly didn't need to come now. I just called to let Tyler know there was a letter here."

Tyler looked around. "Where is it?"

Mrs. Jennings pointed toward the table. Tyler tore into it. Everyone else stood silently, waiting.

"Dear Mr. Jennings," he stopped. "Isn't that cool? I'm Mr. Jennings now."

"Keep going, keep going," said Jacie.

"Thank you for applying to the University of Colorado at Boulder. We have been fortunate to receive many qualified applications this year. Unfortunately . . ." Tyler's voice faded. Hannah held her breath.

Tyler looked up. "I didn't get in."

A stunned silence filled the room.

"I'm sorry, Ty," Becca whispered.

Hannah watched Tyler's face drain of color. Going to this school was all he'd been talking about. She couldn't imagine how devastated he must be.

The letter drifted to the floor.

"How could I not get in?"

chapter 7

The group settled into their spot at the Copperchino. Hannah had never seen Tyler look so down. He hadn't said a word since Becca had suggested coming here instead of going to The Edge. They sipped their drinks in silence, until Solana broke the quiet.

"What other schools did you apply to?" she asked.

Tyler shook his head.

"Don't tell me Boulder was the only one," Becca said. "What about your safeties?"

Tyler leaned back in the leather chair and stared at the ceiling. Hannah wondered if it was to hide the tears in his eyes. "I didn't need safeties. Boulder was a shoo-in. My interview went great. Mom said my essays were flawless—and she's a writer. Besides, it's the only school I've ever wanted to go to. What was the point of applying to others?"

"Maybe in case you didn't get in," Solana muttered.

Jacie shot her a glare and then turned to Tyler. "What do you think you'll do next?"

Ty shrugged like he had when the girls had offered apologies and hugs back at the house, trying to let it all roll off. The girls knew he didn't want pity, but right now they didn't know what else to offer.

"The only option I have is community college, I guess."

"That won't be so bad," Jacie said. "I've heard a lot of people really like it."

Tyler looked up, his eyes stormy. "I know you want me to feel better, but let's be realistic. If I were to go to the CC, my dad would never let me rent an apartment when our house is easy driving distance from school. 'That would be a waste of money,' he'd say."

Jacie put a comforting hand on his shoulder. "You can leave home next year."

Tyler leaned forward, his hands clasped in front of him. "What if they just got my application mixed up? Maybe there's another Tyler Jennings out there who got accepted but wasn't supposed to."

Hannah highly doubted the theory. She'd been praying that God would give her wisdom in how to deal with this situation. Much like Solana's disappointment over Ramón, she truly believed there was some reason behind it. *After all, God, You're in control of everything.* Maybe that's how God was using her words, like Dinah said. She could help Tyler understand God's ways.

A thought struck her. "Maybe God's teaching you something," she blurted out.

"Oh, no." Solana rolled her eyes. "Here we go."

"Like what?" Tyler asked.

"Maybe school became more important than God. Maybe He wants you to get your priorities straight."

"So you think God would cause me not to get in just because I haven't had my devotions in a while?" Tyler looked flustered.

"Think about it. God works everything out for good for those who love Him. So if we show how much we love Him, everything works out. Right?"

"You mean if I loved God more, I would have gotten into CU-Boulder?" Tyler sounded skeptical.

"Or maybe not getting in is God doing what's best for you."

"That's crazy. How could staying around here and going to community college be what's best for me? They don't even have my major."

"But look at the people in the Bible and how they were blessed for being obedient: David became king, Joseph became a ruler, Abraham was prosperous. It's all over the Bible. God blesses those who obey."

Becca looked thoughtful. "It seems a little extreme, but I sort of agree. I remember studying the different kings of Israel. Those who obeyed God were victorious in battle and those who didn't, weren't."

Hannah nodded.

Jacie pulled her knees up to her face and rested her chin between them. "But what about things like me and my dad? You guys know I hate the distance between us. Is that because of my disobedience to God?"

Hannah took a deep breath. The others all looked at her. "Maybe it's because of your dad's disobedience to God." Jacie's dad wasn't a Christian, and Hannah knew things would be different between him and Jacie if they shared the same faith.

"Aha!" Tyler jerked up. "So maybe my rejection from CU-Boulder isn't because of my disobedience but the disobedience of some admissions personnel at the school."

Solana rubbed her temples. "This is getting more and more

confusing. And you all are acting downright weird. Why does everything have to be caused by God? Isn't it all logical? Tyler doesn't have the best GPA in the world, so maybe he just didn't meet the school's criteria. Jacie's dad lives a thousand miles away and is self-absorbed, so that's why he doesn't call that often."

Hannah looked at Jacie for some help, but it seemed like the girl was somewhere in another world, her eyes downcast.

Solana must've noticed, too. "Sorry, Jacie. I didn't mean to call your dad self-absorbed."

Jacie shook her head and let out a breath—that short, shaky breath she'd take when she was trying not to cry. "It's okay. I was just thinking." She paused. "I was just thinking my parents got pregnant out of wedlock—you all know that. And that's dis-obedience to God, right?"

Hannah nodded her head slowly, not liking the direction this was going.

Jacie continued, "And I was born out of that mistake. So does that mean I was never supposed to be?"

"Of course not!" Solana said. "What would we do without you?"

But Jacie's eyes were on Hannah, waiting.

"God knew you'd be born. He's planned everyone's life," Hannah said. She wished she wasn't put on the spot like this. She could see Jacie's point but didn't like the conclusion that came out of it. She needed some time to think about it.

"God knew I'd be born, but I was still a result of disobedi-ence. So does that mean that everything I do won't be right because of someone else's disobedience?"

"Don't be silly, Jacie. Of course God wanted you here," Tyler said.

"Yeah, and we're glad you're here, too," Becca added.

"God can use you no matter what." Hannah said the first thing that came to mind.

Jacie gave a quick close-mouthed smile, but Hannah knew they'd only made her feel worse.

Failure: *The act of really wanting to help your friends but ending up only making them feel like garbage.*

● ● ●

"Could you please put this on the table, Hannah?" Mrs. Connor handed her daughter a big wooden bowl overflowing with a crisp garden salad.

Hannah placed it in the middle of the table and arranged the dressings around it. She could hear Uncle Greg playing with Sarah, Elijah, and Daniel in the living room. When Sarah was being tickled, her laughter burbled joyfully throughout the house.

Dinah was sitting on the floor stringing beads with Rebekah and telling her about how the Native Americans made jewelry. She looked up at Hannah.

"Are you doing okay, Hannah? You seem pretty quiet tonight."

"Yeah, I'm fine. Did you want water or tea?"

"Water, please. Are you sure?"

Hannah knew she couldn't keep things from her aunt. "We can talk about it later."

"Dinnertime!" her mother called as she carried a platter piled high with roast beef, potatoes, and vegetables into the dining room.

"Oh, that looks wonderful, Gretchen," Dinah praised.

"And smells heavenly," added Greg, entering with one twin hanging off each muscular arm like giant purses.

The rest of the family gathered in the small dining room.

"Hannah, look at my new necklace!" said Rebekah.

"I just got a new high score," announced Micah, sitting down with his video game remote still in hand.

"I think I'm going to need to replace the gutters, Greg. Didn't you do yours last year?" said Mr. Connor.

"Would Play-Doh taste good if I put ketchup on it?" asked Sarah.

"Mom, Sarah put one of her doll dresses on my robot and he's a boy!" said Elijah.

Ten faces, five different conversations, and one cross-dressing robot crowded around the big oak table, taking in the steaming dinner.

"Okay," called Mr. Connor above the din. "Who's going to say the blessing?"

"Me, me, me!" Sarah Ruth raised her hand.

"Go ahead, honey. Remember to pray for Aunt Dinah's and Uncle Greg's trip."

"Dear Jesus, thank You for Sherlock our dog and my toys and my bed and my toothbrush and Daniel's toys—especially the robot. She's cool—"

"He! It's a he!" interrupted Elijah.

"And please help Aunt Dinah and Uncle Greg get to Africa and be safe and wear their seat belts on the plane and not get in a fight with any lions. Amen."

"Thank you, Sarah Ruth," said Dinah.

"Oh, I forgot!" Sarah squeezed her eyes tight. "And thank You, God, for this food and the hands that repaired it. Amen."

"That's one way of looking at it," laughed Mrs. Connor.

Hannah enjoyed the food, her family, the fun, and laughter that bounced from one end of the table to the other. But she felt weighted by the events of the last couple days, and she couldn't even figure out which one bothered her most. She felt horrible that Tyler hadn't gotten into his choice school and hurt that she couldn't say anything to cheer him up. And, in the process, she'd hurt Jacie's feelings and made her doubt her very existence. But, worst of all, she found herself replaying the events in the park yesterday. *I'm thinking we should change your nickname from "Holy Hannah" to "Hypocritical Hannah."* It hadn't been a big deal, right? Just a snotty girl making fun of her. But her mind continued to go back to it. *I need to grow up and get over it.*

● ● ●

"You seemed distracted tonight," Aunt Dinah said.

She and Hannah swayed on the back porch swing while Greg and Rebekah took care of the dishes.

Hannah loved these times with her aunt. For some reason she felt like she could share more in the dark, as though her selfish thoughts didn't sound so bad in the evening. And tradition dictated that Hannah and her aunt would have "girltime" on the back porch whenever Dinah visited. They'd been doing it for years. She'd been four when her aunt had commenced the tradition.

Micah had been celebrating his second birthday. Family had gathered around, and everyone wanted to give him attention. Micah, of course, entertained himself more with cake frosting and wrapping paper than the toy cars and stuffed animals hidden inside the packages. Each time he messily unwrapped them with someone else's "help," Hannah would grab the gift. "May I have this one?" she'd always ask.

"No, that's Micah's," her mom would answer.

Feeling rejected, Hannah hid herself in the front closet. It felt like she'd been tucked away in there for hours, but Dinah insisted it was two minutes at the most.

"Hannah," she said as she opened the door, spreading light onto the little girl's tear-stained face. "What are you doing in here?"

"No one likes me," Hannah had said. "I didn't get any gifts."

Dinah nodded, then extended her hand. "I know of one. But it's a big, secret surprise. You have to come with me."

Hannah eagerly latched herself onto her aunt. "Is it from you?"

"Nope."

"Mom and Dad?"

"Not them either."

"Grandma?"

"You'll never guess."

By this time she'd led Hannah onto the back porch. "Now, let's see if we can find it."

Hannah began looking under the porch swing and around the potted plants. "Where is it?"

"You're looking in the wrong spot. Come here." She sat on the swing and held out her arms. Hannah crawled inside.

"Look up at the sky."

Stars littered the clear sky like a ticker-tape parade on New Year's Eve.

"Where?" Hannah asked.

"You get to pick out your own star."

Hannah stared wide-eyed at her aunt. "I do? My very own?"

"Yep. Any one you want."

Hannah unwrapped herself from her aunt's arms and ran out in the middle of the yard to get a better look. Her aunt followed her laughing. "Is it from Uncle Wyatt?"

"Nope. It's from God."

Of course. Who else would be big enough to give such a gift?

Hannah spotted it. The biggest, brightest star in the sky. Later she'd learned it was the North Star. "That one. I want that one."

"It's yours," Dinah said. "You can even name it. Should it be 'Sparkles'?"

Hannah shook her head, flinging her pigtails. She'd thought hard. It would have to be nice. What was the nicest name she could think of?

"Owen," she'd said decisively.

"Owen?"

"He's in my play group. He always shares his toys."

Dinah had nodded. "Of course. Owen."

Dinah and Hannah still laughed at that story. But Hannah always looked for "Owen" first. She wouldn't tell her aunt this, but to this very day she felt like it was the star God had given her.

Hannah smiled at the memory. But she wasn't four anymore. And life had become far more complicated. "Solana's dealing with a really tough breakup and Tyler got turned down from his college and Jacie's still having problems with her dad. And I'm doing a horrible job being a friend."

"Wait a minute." Dinah patted Hannah's knee. "What do you mean you're doing a horrible job?"

"I don't know what to say to them. I want to encourage them and show them that God's plan is bigger and better, but I don't know how. So they're just sad. And someone hurt my feelings today and it shouldn't even matter because everyone else has much worse problems than I do. But if I can't get over my own hurt feelings, how can I help anyone else get over theirs?"

Dinah nodded. "Hannah, you've got to stop."

"What?"

"Trying to be a Super Christian. It's okay to not know what to do. And it's certainly okay to feel hurt and alone. I feel it all the time."

"How could you feel that way? Your life is perfect." As soon as she said it, she remembered Aunt Dinah's life wasn't always as ideal as it seemed now.

"Nope. Not perfect. Not ever. I'll admit, God has blessed me in amazing ways. I have a wonderful husband, great friends, and, of course, the world's best niece."

"Of course," Hannah grinned.

"But, Greg doesn't always understand me exactly the way I want him to. We still miscommunicate; friends still hurt me. I'm still afraid of failure, of not being good enough. I'm terrified of being a mom."

Hannah's eyes widened. She had no idea her aunt had such doubts.

Dinah continued, "And I think God's okay with that. If my life were perfect and I felt complete and knew how to handle every situation, I wouldn't need Him. I wouldn't crave His love and His truth."

"So you think God gives us hard things so we learn to need Him?" Hannah thought back to Kassidy's hateful eyes, Tyler's fallen face when he read the rejection letter, Jacie's tear-streaked cheeks and wadded Kleenex.

"I think we have to be careful with that. Sometimes struggles are the attacks of the devil; other times they are just the result of living in a fallen world—a part of life. But the awesome thing is that God can use every difficulty to bring us closer to Him. He can redeem anything."

"Uh, oh." Hannah smiled. "Here comes the 'redemption spiel.'"

Dinah was always talking about God's ability to make great things come out of bad. But Hannah couldn't blame her. After all, Dinah had lived out that process and knew it firsthand.

Hannah tilted her head. "Do you think there's redemptive work in everything?"

"I believe that as long as we're seeking the heart of God there is. I think God is at work in your and your friends' situations, although that's pretty hard to hear in the middle of a tough time. He can ultimately do good things out of any of those, but I can't say that He willed them to be. In fact, I think God is probably grieving that Jacie's dad disappointed her again, because Jacie is His daughter and He knows how much this means to her."

"But then you're saying God doesn't have control over everything."

"No, I'm not saying that. I'm saying that sometimes God allows people to make their own choices from which bad things happen, even if it makes Him very sad. And then, there are the times when people make good choices and bad things still happen. I don't understand it, Hannah, and I never will. All I know is God is all-powerful, all-knowing, and He's good."

Hannah weighed those words. She'd always imagined God as watching her from heaven. If she were obedient, He'd reward her and life would be pleasant. But if she messed up, He'd punish her somehow to bring her back into obedience. But this talk—well, it didn't make sense. To have difficult things happen even when she was doing everything she could to follow God?

A sprinkler tick-tick-ticked one direction in the neighbor's yard. Then it sputtered all the way back to the starting point.

The verse she'd shared with Tyler last night popped into Hannah's head. "But the Bible says in Romans 8:28 that all things work together for good if we love God."

"True," Dinah nodded. "But that promise doesn't keep us from pain. All things do *ultimately* work together for good, but sometimes there's a journey of a whole lot of bad before we get there."

Hannah felt an unsettled feeling in the pit of her stomach. For some reason, she didn't like this conversation. It made God seem so volatile, so unpredictable. She wanted to believe that there was an understandable reason for everything. She longed to tell Jacie and Tyler and Solana wise words that would clear up their doubt, fear, and hurt. But she didn't know what those words would be. She didn't know what God was doing. And the whole Kassidy situation had redirected all the energy she should be using to figure it out.

"But what about the scriptures that say 'the prayers of a righteous man availeth much' or that our faith can move mountains? Don't you think some things happen because we don't pray enough, or have enough faith?" she asked.

"Those verses are very true. But we can't use them to control God and manipulate our situations. God is God, whether we understand Him or not. Don't try to put Him into a box. He won't go there."

What kind of answer was that? It didn't help her with any of her questions. "That doesn't help me explain to my friends why bad things happen," she muttered.

"I don't know if I would count on always being able to explain things. Sometimes we just have to walk through what life is throwing at us, and figure out what it's about later. And we may never figure it out before we get to heaven."

Why did God have to be so confusing?

Dinah placed her hand over Hannah's. "Just be a friend, Hannah."

"I'm trying."

"I know you are," Dinah said. "And you're a good friend. But remember, God is God, and He made you to be Hannah."

● ● ●

Hannah couldn't sleep that night. It had been so good to have her aunt and uncle visit. Dinner had been crazy and loud and so much fun. Greg had everyone cracking up with his stories of the pranks his youth group pulled on him.

And she'd loved the minutes she'd been able to get away with her aunt and just talk. But she felt an ache of disappointment. She'd wanted her aunt to encourage her to be strong, to pray harder, to give her something tangible to take back to her friends, to do something . . . anything. But this whole waiting-it-out, God-doesn't-make-sense thing left her feeling . . . well . . . incomplete.

Her aunt had given her a big hug good-bye. "Good things are yet to come," she'd said. Hannah hoped she was right. *Of course she is.* She snuggled her head deeper into the pillow. *Things will get better.*

chapter 8

"So now we pour this chemical into the flask on the Bunsen burner."

"Go ahead," Hannah said to Galvin.

Galvin peered at her through his lab goggles. "But you've hardly had a chance to do anything. C'mon, this is the crux of the experiment."

"I'm fine taking notes." The truth was Hannah had a phobia of chemistry experiments. She wasn't known for being the most graceful person, and it was moments like this when a steady hand and good balance were of utmost importance that she'd find herself tripping over her own feet, sprawled on the floor with dangerous chemicals burning off her leg. "Really, go ahead."

Galvin shrugged and tipped the test tube over the burner, letting the liquid slowly drip into the flask.

Hannah suspected chemistry was one of the reasons her

parents decided to send her to public school last year. When she'd taken a class with other homeschoolers in Michigan a couple years ago, she'd ended up burning Mrs. Parrott's new wood kitchen floor. It hadn't been *too* bad, but Mrs. Parrott asked Mrs. Connor to teach Hannah chemistry in their own home.

"Are you going to the basketball game tomorrow night?" Galvin asked.

"Yes. One of my good friends, Becca McKinnon, is starting."

"I know Becca. She's pretty cool. So is her boyfriend. Nate and I have shot hoops a few times."

Hannah nodded.

"I guess I noticed you hanging around her."

Hannah glanced at him out of the corner of her eye, pretending to be absorbed in jotting down notes.

"I've kinda noticed you for a while, y'know."

Hannah scribbled furiously. "Yeah, it should be a good game Tuesday."

"So, since you're going and I'm going, maybe we could go together."

Hannah's heart started to race. "I don't think so."

"Why not?"

She put down her pencil and turned to look at Galvin. "Because that would pretty much be a date, and my parents and I have decided that I don't need to be in dating relationships while I'm in high school. We believe in courtship."

Galvin's brow wrinkled. "I'd heard that about you. But you seemed pretty interested in me when I asked about being your lab partner."

Hannah let out a slow breath. How was she going to explain this one? "Well, it's not like I have anything against you as a person. You seem really nice." *Nice? Guys hate that.* Jacie and Tyler were always reminding her not to say that to a guy.

She tried to dig herself out. "And you're certainly attractive." Galvin's eyes widened. *Maybe that was a bit too much.* "Having you for a lab partner is fine, but I couldn't have any further relationship with you."

"Because of your whole courtship thing."

"Yes." Good. He understood. Awkward moment over.

"So if you didn't believe in courtship, would I be the kind of guy you'd date?"

"That's irrelevant. Because I do."

"But what if you didn't?"

Hannah went back to her notes. "I would only date Christians."

"I'm a Christian."

"Who go to strong, Bible-believing churches."

"I go to a Bible church. Every week."

"And come from good, morally upstanding families."

"That's my family, all right."

Hannah racked her brain. She already knew Galvin was intelligent, courteous, and kind. "Well . . . then maybe you would be. But it's not even an issue because I *do* believe in courtship and that's the end of the conversation, isn't it?"

Galvin smirked at her, like he was going to laugh any second.

"What?" she demanded.

"Nothing, nothing at all." He shook his head, the annoying smile still plastered across his face. "End of conversation, remember?"

"Glad you're having such an amusing chat Mr. Parker, and Ms. . . . uh . . . Hannah," Dr. Hanson called from his desk. "But perhaps we should save our tête-à-tête for a Friday night date and . . . uh . . . do our experiment now. Please."

The entire class turned to look at Hannah. Kassidy's friends giggled. Kassidy did not.

"Yes, sir," Galvin half-laughed. "No more tête-à-tête."

What? He was only increasing the rumor mill ammunition. "But we're not technically having a tête-à-tête," Hannah announced. "Just a conversation."

"I see." Dr. Hanson rescued his slipping glasses. "But I'm guessing from the laughter that the conversation wasn't pertaining to chemistry. Unless, of course, your experiment happens to be more humorous than the others." It was a line Dr. Hanson had down pat. He used it all the time. Probably practiced saying it in his bathroom mirror with just the right amount of sternness.

"Yes, sir," Hannah echoed. *Just please get the attention off me.*

"Yes, sir," Galvin said.

● ● ●

Hannah's eyes ached from staring at the computer screen so long, but she'd finally perfected her first few pictures of homecoming week. *These will look great in the layout.* The cartoon stallion mascot rearing and ready to establish dominance. Laughing girls with painted faces. The marching band in formation. *I'm going to have too many pictures by the end of the week.* But she knew she'd rather have an overabundance than not enough. She adjusted the pixels one more time and looked at her watch. She should be heading out to meet her friends in the quad pretty soon. The girls had decided to go shopping again today for Jacie's dress. She started laying out photos in a mock format, when she sensed someone watching her. Turning, she found Kassidy Jordan standing in the doorway of the lab.

"Hi, Kassidy." She forced a friendly smile.

"You don't have to play games with me, Hannah," Kassidy said, pulling a chair from beneath a desk and seating herself prissily at the edge of it. She crossed her legs and drummed her fingers on her knees. "I know where we stand."

"Can I help you with something?"

"How about starting with the truth?"

Hannah raised her eyebrows. "I'm sorry. I don't know what you mean."

"I really don't give a rip if the entire school thinks you're little Miss Perfect, but I pride myself in being pretty well-informed. So I'm not asking you to change, Hannah. I just want to know the real story behind that supposed innocence of yours."

Kassidy reminded Hannah of lawyer dramas on television. Articulate and confident, Kassidy must have watched a number of them in order to get her intimidation factor just right.

"Kassidy, honestly, I have no interest in Galvin." This whole thing frustrated Hannah to no end. How could she convince this girl that Galvin was a pain, not someone she wanted to date?

"Let's look at the facts," Kassidy said.

Yep, future lawyer for sure.

"Anyone in that room today would have told a very different story. Why do you expect me to believe one thing when your actions clearly show another? I even heard you talking about dating."

"I was telling him I *don't* date . . ." Hannah said, knowing that wouldn't convince anyone believing a lie.

"Well, maybe you should start *acting* like you don't date." Kassidy stood up. "I'm done playing these games, Hannah. You haven't been at this school very long, but you know the rules. And when a guy is interested in someone—especially someone like me—other girls don't start getting in the way strutting their stuff."

"I wasn't . . . strutting." Hannah's voice faltered. Was she inadvertently doing something like that? She'd accidentally flirted with a boy named Brendan before. Maybe she was doing it again. She felt horrified. What did *strutting* look like?

"So just consider us at odds. And, you probably know this, too: You don't want to be at odds with me."

● ● ●

"How's the Galvin experiment going, Solana?" asked Jacie. She shoved her keys into her purse while she, Becca, Hannah, and Solana navigated around cars in the strip mall parking lot.

"I didn't see him today, except when he was walking down the hall with Miss Hannah here," said Solana, staring pointedly at Hannah.

"We were talking about our experiment as we were leaving class," Hannah explained. That was mostly true. He'd been trying to start up a conversation with her about her interests, but she kept going back to chemicals and other safe topics.

"Can we stop in Raggs real quick so I can pick up my check?" asked Jacie. The others agreed. The boutique was right on the way to the department store.

Solana linked arms with Hannah. "Well, maybe the next time you chat in chemistry you can mention something about me. Like—"

"Oh no. I told you I didn't want a part in this." She didn't want to have to explain how complicated things had become with Galvin. "Kassidy Jordan already has it out for me just for being his lab partner."

"That's really strange that she would be so protective of him. You're just doing a chemistry experiment together," Becca said.

Hannah grunted an agreement. She didn't want to say too much. Obviously Solana's experiment wasn't going too well if she continued to nag Hannah about helping her out. And right now, she wanted Galvin Parker as far away from her as possible. She couldn't wait for the chemistry experiment to be over.

Jacie gestured toward the display window in front of the store, her voice wistful. "There's the dress."

Hannah gasped as she laid eyes on a beautiful blue gown. Form-fitting on top with spaghetti straps, the shimmery, sheer material flowed into an asymmetrical hem, one side exposing the knee. It was soft and elegant and beautiful and . . .

"Sexy!" said Solana. "I love it!"

"It's beautiful," said Becca, taking the word out of Hannah's mouth.

"Did you try it on?" asked Solana.

Jacie nodded. "Like three times. I love it. But I can't get it. It costs way too much."

Hannah strained to see the price tag. "Yikes!" *Maybe if the decimal point were one digit to the left—*

"That's why I'll be wearing last year's dress."

"But you're on the homecoming court! You might even be queen! You have to wear something special!" insisted Solana.

Jacie shrugged. "Not if I can't afford it."

"I wish I had time to make you something," said Hannah.

The door dinged a welcome as they entered the shop. Loud dance music bounced off the walls while a handful of girls sifted through the racks.

"It's a slow day," said Becca over the pounding beat.

Jacie nodded. "It's been that way lately."

An older lady with platinum blonde hair and a pair of spectacles dangling from a chain around her neck ran up to Jacie. "Oh, dear, I'm so glad you're here. I was meeting with some advertising people this week and I wanted to get your opinion on a couple things."

"Sure, Mrs. Gumphrey. These are my friends: Solana, Becca, and Hannah." Jacie turned to her friends. "Mrs. Gumphrey owns the store."

"Hello, dears," she said. She glanced their way, and then did a double take. The woman looked Hannah up and down. "Would you like a job?" she asked.

"What?" Hannah asked.

"As a live mannequin. We'll be starting a new promotion next week. Instead of having plastic mannequins in the display windows, we'll have live models wearing the clothes." She walked around Hannah like she was a piece of livestock up for sale. "And you've got the perfect figure—tall, slender, nice curves."

Hannah put her hands over her rear self-consciously. "Um, no thanks." She couldn't think of a worse job than standing in a window all day wearing who-knows-what, while people gawked at you. And what would her parents think?

Mrs. Gumphrey shook her head. "I usually don't have to try such gimmicks, but I need to do something that gets attention. They've opened two new clothing stores in this shopping center—just this season—that cater to the same crowd I do. I need to set myself apart somehow."

"It seems like you're doing well. All the girls at school shop here," said Solana.

Mrs. Gumphrey fingered her glasses. "Yes, and if they all wore signs on their backs saying, 'From Raggs by Razz,' that would be all the publicity I'd need. But that's not happening."

An idea struck Hannah. "You know what would be perfect? If you could somehow advertise your clothes at homecoming this week. Everyone will be at the game on Friday night when they announce the homecoming court."

Jacie raised her eyebrows and exchanged a quizzical glance with Becca.

"So what should I do? Wave a banner from the stands?" asked Mrs. Gumphrey.

"No. Convince one of the girls in the homecoming court to wear a dress from your shop. Lend it to her for the evening at no charge, and then when they announce the queen nominees with their escorts, they can say the dress is courtesy of Raggs by Razz."

Jacie winked at Hannah, and Solana gave her a subtle nod of approval. Mrs. Gumphrey chewed on the end of her spectacles and stared into nowhere.

She turned back to Hannah. "That, my dear, is a brilliant idea! Would you be able to tell me who's in the court this year?"

"Well . . . Jacie, for one."

"Jacie? That's wonderful!" She turned to Jacie, who beamed from ear to ear. "Congratulations, dear. But I shouldn't get ahead of myself. Would you mind doing this young lady's idea? Is there a dress that you'd like to wear?"

Jacie grinned. "As a matter of fact, there is."

Success: *Making a friend's day.*

chapter 9

"Hey, Galvin." Kassidy sidled up against the lab table.

Hannah pretended to be absorbed in her note-taking, but she watched the interaction out of the corner of her eye. Kassidy leaned in closer to Galvin, giving him her shimmery-lipped smile and playfully batting her eyes.

So that's how you're supposed to do it.

"Everyone was so bummed that you couldn't make it the other night when we were hanging out." She stuck her lower lip out in a pathetic pout.

"Yeah, sorry about that. Did you have a good time?"

"Galvin, we *always* have a good time." She laughed, forced and fake. Hannah wanted to gag. Kassidy's giggle was *so* annoying. "You should definitely join us next time. In fact, we're having a party at Lindsey's house on Saturday. It should be a blast."

"Maybe."

Hannah realized she was writing *Bunsen burner* repeatedly

all over her notes. *What were Galvin's observations on that last step?* Shoot, she'd have to ask him again and then he'd know she wasn't really paying attention. The conversation had stopped and she noticed Galvin jerking his head in Hannah's direction.

"What?" Kassidy asked, her voice hushed.

Galvin's words came through clenched teeth. "If we're talking about it in front of Hannah, you should invite her."

Oh, yeah. Real subtle, Galvin.

"Hannah?!" Kassidy shrieked, and then let out an over-the-top laugh.

Oh, great.

"What's so funny?" Galvin said.

"Hannah," Kassidy repeated. She turned to Hannah. "Have you explained to Galvin that you don't do parties?"

Hannah didn't know what to say. "I don't do *those* kinds of parties," corrected Hannah.

"I stand corrected. Hannah will do knitting parties, church potluck parties, and who-can-dress-the-most-like-a-blind-grandma parties," Kassidy shot back. "Hannah wouldn't be interested in a party like this because she doesn't believe in fun. She's too busy waiting for some missionary to come and marry her so they can go teach Bible studies together."

Hannah just stared at Kassidy, her mouth agape.

Kassidy patted Hannah's hand. "It's okay, Hannah. I'm sorry to upset you with talk of people dancing and being loud and—oh no!—drinking!"

Galvin looked from Kassidy to Hannah and back to Kassidy again. "I don't do drinking parties either."

Kassidy's cheeks reddened slightly, but she recovered quickly with a casual shrug. "Well, not everyone drinks. I don't." She smiled her famous bright smile and tilted her head to one side, then reached up and slid her finger along Galvin's chin. "Think about it. Let me know."

She sauntered away, with an expert swing in her hips.

Hannah felt the tears spring to her eyes and started scribbling on her notes before Galvin noticed them. *It's not a big deal,* she told herself. *So what if Kassidy humiliated me in front of Galvin. I don't care what he thinks anyway. It doesn't bother me that much. This is just silly.* She wrote faster, feeling like everyone must be watching her—especially Kassidy. *My face must be beet red. Why do I have to blush so easily?*

Galvin's voice came from beside her right shoulder. "I think you made your point that we used a Bunsen burner."

Hannah looked down at her paper.

"I'm sorry about that," Galvin continued. "She was really rude."

"It's not a big deal. I don't care."

He peered at her. "Are you crying?"

"No." Hannah swallowed. "Maybe it's the chemicals."

Galvin nodded. "Of course."

"I missed that last observation. What did you say about step nine?"

"You're kind of cute when you're about to cry."

Haven't I been embarrassed enough already? "What's the observation, Galvin?"

"Element turned a yellowish color upon boiling."

"Thank you."

"Now we're adding the next chemical."

Hannah turned a page in her notebook.

"So what if you don't drink?" he said, pouring in the contents of the test tube. "I think that's pretty cool. A lot of people would think that's cool. You don't need to get upset that one person disagrees with you."

"I'm not upset. I don't care what Kassidy thinks. I don't care what *anyone* thinks." She knew her words came out sharper than she intended, but she couldn't help it.

"Don't get upset with me." He put his palms up in mock surrender. "I'm just trying to be your friend."

"Sorry," she mumbled, staring at her notes.

"That's okay, isn't it?" Galvin asked. "I mean, that we're friends. It seems like when we talked that first day you were really nice and open, but since then . . . well . . . you sort of treat me like I have the plague."

How could she explain this one? *I was trying to get rid of you the first day I met you and that's why I was so nice.* He wouldn't understand she couldn't get all chummy with him, even if she did think he was a nice guy. What would everyone else think? Her own words came back to her: *I don't care what anyone thinks.* So maybe that wasn't exactly true. But she did have to maintain some sort of reputation. People knew she was a Christian. They expected her to act like someone who lived out a belief in courtship. And Galvin should realize that, shouldn't he? She'd explained it to him yesterday.

Hannah took a deep breath. "I told you before, I believe in courtship."

"I know. But what does that have to do with us just hanging out?"

Smoke began pouring out of the beaker. Hannah jotted the result down in her notebook before responding.

"So then you can understand why I like to keep a distance from attractive men."

Oops.

"Oh." Galvin grinned and then forced his mouth downward. "I see."

"Can we clean up now?" she asked.

"Yeah. But that doesn't mean you can't hang out with guys, right? I mean, you obviously hang out with Tyler Jennings. Or maybe you don't consider him . . ."

Hannah cut him off before he could repeat the word *attrac-*

tive. "Tyler and I only hang out in a group, usually with three other girls. I'm not giving him the wrong impression."

"So are you worried you're giving *me* the wrong impression?"

The bell rang. "I'm just being cautious," she insisted. "Now we need to clean up. We're late." *Just let me out of here.*

"Why can't we just hang out then? As friends. With your friends," he said. "C'mon, I'm the new kid. I'm trying to find my niche."

Solana would love for you to find your niche with us, Hannah thought. She could relate to being the new kid. It wasn't fun coming into a big school where everyone already had their own friends.

She took a deep breath. "Sure, you can hang out with us, but I want to make something really clear."

"What?"

"I'm not interested in you. So don't try to talk me into a relationship."

Galvin laughed. "Okay, already." He backed up with his hands lifted as if in surrender. "I promise I won't stalk you."

Hannah knew she was pouring it on a little thick, but she didn't want any misunderstandings. She'd had enough of those.

"If you want, join us at the game tonight. We usually sit near the top of the bleachers in the middle section."

"I'll be there."

● ● ●

"Go, Becca!"

The whistle blew. The referee threw the ball up and Becca sprung into the air, elevating herself over her opponent. She tipped the ball to her teammate and the Stony Brook side of the gym erupted into cheers.

"That's my girl," yelled Nate, clapping his hands.

Hannah fazed out from the game. She loved attending, but it was mostly because she loved getting all hyper with her friends, not because she cared about basketball. It was kind of fun to yell as loudly as she could and still not be able to hear her voice.

"Go, Becca!" she shouted, just to prove her own point.

"Yay, Becca!" Jacie shouted beside her.

Nate sat on her other side, nervously rolling a plastic-wrapped bouquet of flowers between his palms. He always got Becca flowers to give to her after the game. By the looks of it, they wouldn't be in very good shape by the end of the fourth quarter, but Becca wouldn't notice. She'd just wrap her arms around Nate's neck and he'd spin her around so her legs flailed out. Well, if they won, at least. If they lost, he'd put his arm around her shoulder and she'd lean into his chest.

Hannah was content not to date and knew it was the right decision for her, but she'd often watch Nate and Becca, thinking, *Someday, I'd like a relationship like that.* The two just matched. They weren't *loco* over each other, to use Solana's term, but they really enjoyed being together. It seemed like they spoke a different language that only the two of them understood. And Hannah knew they were each other's biggest prayer warriors.

Nate let out a whoop, letting Hannah know Becca was doing something amazing.

She watched Becca steal the ball from a Green Mountain player and race up the court. She passed to Kristin Andersen, who passed it to Lindsey Sutton. Hannah saw Becca get open under the basket, waving her arms. Lindsey shot at the hoop, but the ball bounced off the rim. Like a rocket, Becca was skyward, grabbing the ball and swishing it through the net. The Stony Brook crowd roared to their feet.

"Did you see that? Did you see that?!" Nate shouted.

Becca ran down court, guarding a Green Mountain girl

who looked about twice her size. The ball bounced past Becca toward the Green Mountain giant. Becca's hand popped out, nabbing the ball before the opposing player could get her hands on it. She raced back to the Stony Brook side.

"Five . . . four . . . three . . ." the crowd chanted, as the seconds ticked down to the end of the second quarter. Still far from the basket, Becca threw the ball into the air. The world seemed to move in slow motion as the ball floated toward the basket in the suddenly silent gym. *Boing.* The ball lightly bounced off the right side of the rim. *Boing.* It hit the left. *Bzzzzzz.* The buzzer sounded. The ball rolled around the front of the rim and sank inside.

The Stony Brook side of the gym exploded. A hundred blue-and-gold pom-poms shimmied in the air.

"A three-pointer!" screamed Nate.

The rest of the *Brio* group cheered with the other ecstatic fans. The bleachers shook as Nate jumped up and down, the poor flowers leaning their heads pathetically over their stems. He waved the mangled bunch wildly over his head, trying to get Becca's attention. The teams were heading into the locker rooms. Hannah noticed Becca scanning the wild crowd. When she saw Nate, a huge grin lit up her face and she waved back.

"You're on fire!" yelled Nate. There's no way Becca could hear him, but she gave a thumbs-up sign in response.

"That girl is on fire tonight!" Nate repeated to anyone who wanted to listen.

"Could you believe that shot?" Tyler gave Nate a high-five. "Your coaching did some good."

"I can't take any credit," Nate said.

"Let's grab some sodas," Jacie said. "My throat is dry after all that screaming."

"I'm with you," said Solana. "Hey, check it out. Look who's coming this way."

Amidst the sea of fans wandering to restrooms and concession stands came a trim, lanky boy scaling the bleacher steps. Galvin. Hannah had been half watching out for him during the first quarter, but when he hadn't shown up then, she'd been relieved to just enjoy the game and think no more of it. But, here he was.

"Remember, I'm playing it coy," Solana murmured.

"Hi. How are you liking the game?" Galvin said, approaching the group.

"Our girl is beyond awesome," Tyler said. He jumped up and mimed a layup.

Nate opened his mouth and started to say something, but Solana cut him off. "Oh, Galvin, hi," Solana said. "Pretty exciting, hmm?"

Galvin nodded at the verbal barrage, but spoke to the one he stared at with interest. "So what did you think, Hannah?"

Everyone turned to focus on Hannah.

"Uh. Wow. Yeah . . . cool. Three-pointer." *Uh, oh. Solana does not look happy.*

Galvin didn't seem to care about her lame comment. He addressed Tyler, Nate, Solana, and Jacie. "Mind if I sit with you guys during the second half?"

"That'd be cool," Tyler said. "Come get drinks with us."

"I think I'll stay here," Solana said.

"I thought you were thirsty," Jacie said.

"I hate waiting in lines, though."

"I can get something for you," Galvin said.

"Oh, that's sweet," Solana said, a sparkle escaping her eye. "Diet Coke, please."

"Hannah, do you want anything?" Galvin asked.

"No, thanks." Hannah stood up. She suddenly felt hot and stifled. "I'm going to step outside and get some air."

● ● ●

"Bec-ca, Bec-ca, Bec-ca," the crowd chanted as Becca ran out onto the court with her teammates. She started the third quarter still in "a zone," as Nate told anyone who would listen. She was all over the place, stealing balls, making perfect passes. She'd already scored 18 points as the third quarter came to a close.

"That makes her career high," Nate shouted to the *Brio* gang, as she sunk yet another basket.

The crowd began to chant down the last 10 seconds of the third quarter. A teammate passed Becca the ball. She dribbled down the court. The crowd rose in anticipation. Would she pull another three-point buzzer shot? She dodged around the Green Mountain opponent blocking her, only to find another one in her face, double-teaming her. She whipped around the second girl with a clear shot for a layup.

"Five . . . four . . ."

She jumped up toward the basket, seemingly suspended several feet in the air. The Green Mountain guard leapt to tip the ball away from the basket, barely hitting it with her fingers and colliding with Becca in midair. The two landed in a clump on the wooden floor, and the thump of falling bodies echoed through the gym. The ball rolled around the edge and dropped in.

"Becca!" Nate called, hands cupped around his mouth.

The Green Mountain girl stood and brushed herself off.

But Becca remained, her body askew on the floor. Not moving.

chapter 10

"Stand back. We're taking care of her."

The *Brio* gang stood on the edge of the court, watching as paramedics and coaches talked to Becca. Tears streamed down her face. Hannah could now see, at a closer vantage point, the odd twist in Becca's leg. She'd never seen a leg turned backwards before. Becca usually kept a stiff upper lip about everything, but her face contorted in agony as the medics tried to move her twisted knee.

"No!" Becca cried, the pain evident in her voice. Pools of tears settled beside her face on the gym floor.

Hannah felt Nate stiffen beside her.

"Give us some room, kids." The assistant coach began to push the group back. "Get out of the way."

"But this is our friend. We need to help," Hannah insisted.

"The best thing you can do to help is let the medics do their job."

Nate ducked under the man's arms and ran to Becca's side. He gently wiped away the falling tears and took her hand.

A siren wailed closer toward the school.

"Oh, God," Hannah whispered. "Please ease her pain. Please comfort Becca right now. Be with her." She could feel herself on the edge of tears. Was there anything worse than standing by, helpless, while her friend winced with pain?

"I want to do something," Jacie said in Hannah's ear.

"The only thing I can think to do is pray." Hannah's eyes stayed focused on Becca's distraught face.

"Me, too. But I want to do more."

Hannah turned to look at her. Tears poured down Jacie's face and triggered Hannah's. They hugged.

Solana stood next to Hannah, clutching the skinny black strap of her purse. Hannah reached over to take her hand, not knowing if Solana would brush her off or not. She took Jacie's in her other hand. The three girls stood there watching Becca moan and cry, Nate trying to hover over her but the coach pulling him back. *Please, please, God. Help her,* Hannah prayed over and over again. It was a minute before she realized Tyler stood behind them, his hands on Solana's and Jacie's shoulders.

"Move aside, please," a paramedic carrying a stretcher said.

"Excuse me," a frantic voice called from the edges of the crowd.

A dark-haired woman pushed her way through the crowd. "Excuse me. That's my daughter. Excuse me."

She reached the inside circle where the paramedics were strapping Becca onto the stretcher. "I'm her mother. I just got here," she informed them. Her voice sounded businesslike, but Hannah could see the panic on her face.

"Mom," Becca said.

A man took Mrs. McKinnon aside and spoke softly to her.

Mrs. McKinnon nodded, her brows pulled together in intense concentration.

The paramedics lifted the stretcher holding Becca and maneuvered their way through the parting crowd. Each friend reached out to touch Becca as she passed. Her teary eyes watched them, and Hannah thought she saw gratitude mixed with the pain.

Nate followed behind her and stopped in front of the group. His own eyes looked watery. "Her mom's riding with her to the hospital. I'm driving. Let's go."

Without saying anything, the group followed behind him out the doors and into the parking lot. Ambulance lights lit up the long driveway of Stony Brook High and then disappeared.

● ● ●

Hannah paced back and forth along the line of blue chairs at Stony Brook Community Hospital, while the rest of her friends and Galvin formed a huddle in front of her.

"I hate emergency rooms," said Solana, probably flashing back to when her Uncle Manuel had been in this same one.

"Does anyone want anything to drink?" Galvin asked.

Hannah shook her head. She'd almost forgotten he was there. She didn't want him there. He didn't belong. Why had he come anyway?

Hannah had prayed the entire ride to the hospital, crammed between Jacie and Tyler in Nate's backseat. Solana sat in the front talking a mile a minute. "She's going to be absolutely crushed if she can't play basketball. It's her last season. She's co-captain. She's been so excited about this year. And you saw her play tonight; it was going to be her best year yet."

Hannah had become annoyed. She'd known this already. They all knew this, and it was only making them feel worse.

Hannah sat in a stained fabric chair, still trying to find prayers to say on Becca's behalf. And waiting. It seemed they'd been waiting for hours, although the clock above the reception desk claimed they'd only been there 45 minutes.

Mrs. McKinnon finally appeared and sat on a magazine-strewn table in front of the group. She began to speak, her voice weary.

"She's torn ligaments in her knee. Thankfully, nothing's broken. But . . ." She took a deep breath. "She's out for the season. And she'll be on crutches for the next month or so."

Hannah and her friends exchanged glances.

"Wow," Nate said, his body slumping forward. "She must be really upset."

Mrs. McKinnon nodded. "She's going to need all of you to get through this. She'll heal in time, of course, but—"

"Can we see her?" asked Jacie.

"I wish I could say yes, but the hospital staff can't handle all of you being back there. They're going to run a few more X-rays and then we're taking her home. But I know she'd love it if you stopped by after school tomorrow."

The group nodded. Nate looked like he was about to say something and then shut his mouth.

"Thanks for waiting. You're all such good friends to Becca."

Mr. McKinnon rushed through the door, concern written on his face. "Where is she? How is she?"

Mrs. McKinnon pointed down the hall. "Through those doors. Room three." Then she gave each friend a hug before walking down the hall hand in hand with her husband.

"Okay, c'mon, guys," Tyler nodded.

"I can't believe we can't even see her!" Solana said.

"We know she's mostly okay. That's good news," Hannah said.

"Not good enough," said Nate.

● ● ●

The following day at school felt strange. An obvious part of the group was lacking—like a body that one day woke up with only one leg. Even at lunch, Tyler, Hannah, Jacie, and Solana sat in silence, except when Galvin came over to the table.

"Anyone talk to Becca today?" he asked.

"Nate's on the phone with her right now." Tyler nodded toward the doorway, where Nate talked on his cell phone, one hand over his opposite ear to block out the cafeteria noise.

The group had already made a giant "Get Well" card to deliver to Becca—signed by her entire team and most of the seniors. They had cookies and notes to take over, and they planned to pick up flowers and balloons on the way. Hannah and the others had racked their brains trying to come up with anything that would make Becca feel better. But all Hannah could picture was Becca lying in bed, miserable, bemoaning the wasted season ahead of her.

"Well, when you see her, tell her I said I hope she feels better," he said. He watched Hannah, waiting for something. Finally, he turned and walked away.

After Galvin left, Tyler twirled around his soggy fries with a fork. "It sure isn't the year we planned, is it?"

Jacie's chin rested in her hands. "Nope. It doesn't seem like anything is going right."

Hannah stood up and excused herself. "I need to work on the layout, so I should get to the lab. We're meeting right after school to visit Becca, right?"

Everyone nodded.

"Okay, I'll just need to get to the homecoming bonfire tonight to take pictures for an hour or so. Is anyone else planning on going?"

The others declined, saying they'd rather spend the evening at Becca's.

Hannah made her way to the journalism lab. It was true she needed to work on the spread, but more importantly, she wanted to figure out what to do with this weird, awkward sadness. If God was using her to show the others that He was still involved, she wasn't doing a very good job of it. But she didn't know how. She had tried to help with Solana's, Tyler's, and Jacie's problems, and now Becca was in a mess.

God, You have to help me with this. I don't know what to say, she prayed as she played around in Photoshop.

Solana's entrance interrupted her thoughts. "Can I check my e-mail real quick?"

"Sure." Hannah pointed her to a nearby computer. "I thought you checked it earlier."

"I did. I check it about 10 times a day." Solana's fingers flew across the keyboard as she logged on.

"Hoping for a note from Ramón?" Hannah said.

Solana leaned back, waiting. "I guess."

Hannah looked back at the page layout in front of her. She liked Ramón but, in her opinion, Solana was better off without him. But how could she communicate that to Solana in a way she would understand? *Maybe, God, if You just allow him to never e-mail her, she'll finally be able to let go of him. Help her get over him, God.*

Solana gasped. "He wrote! He wrote!"

Okay, God. Just a suggestion.

"What'd he say?" Hannah asked.

Solana ignored her, too engrossed in the words in front of her. "I can't believe this," she said finally, then sniffed. "I can't believe this."

Hannah pulled up a chair next to Solana.

"Read it for yourself," Solana said.

Dear Solana,

You know the last week has been so hard for me, and I know it has been for you, too. I've tried not to e-mail yet because I know it will only keep me attached to you. My heart and mind are still in Copper Ridge with you and I can't afford to do that right now. There are too many other things that are demanding my time and energy. I didn't know it would be this hard to leave you. I hate to say this—hate it more than anything—but I think we need to cut off communication for a while. I need time to settle into this place. You've had such an incredible impact on my life. But I do feel this is what is best for us. I want you to be able to enjoy your senior year without trying to keep a relationship together—a relationship between two people who live in two very different worlds. You have too much spunk in you to sit and wait for the phone to ring every night. I still care for you and want your friendship, but I don't think it's a good idea right now to pursue that. Give me a few months, and I'll give you a call. I promise I won't ever forget you.

—Ramón

"I won't ever forget you," Solana repeated.

"Wow," said Hannah, remembering her quick prayer. *Sometimes, God, You work really fast.*

"A few months?" Solana said. "I feel so stupid. Why can't I just get over him?"

"I thought you were," Hannah said.

"I thought so, too. But I still check my e-mail 10 times a day, hoping he's written. And then he does. And this is what I get!" Solana gestured toward the monitor screen. "'Give me a few months, and I'll give you a call.'"

She hit the reply button and began typing furiously.

"You're not telling him off, are you?" asked Hannah. That would certainly be like Solana. But she'd always been different with Ramón.

"Nope, I wouldn't give him the pleasure," Solana continued to type.

Hannah couldn't resist. She read over Solana's shoulder.

Ramón,

How nice of you to write! Things here are so busy and crazy, time seemed to slip away. I completely agree with you. A girl needs her freedom, so I'm glad you came to that decision. Better to end ties now than later. Glad everything is going well.

—Solana

"How's that?" Solana asked, her cursor on the "send" button.

"It's . . . uh . . . I don't know." *A lie*, she wanted to say. *Completely*. And yet she understood why Solana would want to write it. "Do you think it's a little much?"

"Nope," Solana said. "I think it's perfect." She clicked to send it and stood up. "There, done."

"Are you okay?"

"I'm better than okay. The door is closed. For good, this time."

Hannah remembered Solana saying something similar to that last week. It didn't sound like she meant it any more today than she had then. A guilty itch in her heart made her regret her quickly spoken prayer. Maybe she didn't realize how attached Solana was to Ramón. "Are you sure?"

"Stop being so sensitive. Of course, I'm sure. I'll see you after school." Solana slung her backpack over her shoulder and marched out the door. But Hannah noticed she grabbed a Kleenex on the way out.

● ● ●

Becca lay on the couch with her wrapped leg elevated. Cheery bouquets of flowers and balloons surrounded her. But her face looked pale and withdrawn in comparison. She clumsily joked around with the rest of the group, but Hannah could tell her heart was far away. It made Hannah feel like they were intruding on Becca, instead of comforting her. Maybe this was her chance to spread God's light.

"I've been praying for you, Becca," she said.

"Thanks. Maybe you can pray that my leg heals up by next week so I can play in the game against Valley," Becca said.

"I've been praying more that you would do what God wants you to do during this time," she said.

"And what do you think that might be?" Becca asked.

"Maybe He wants you to spend more time with Him, more time in prayer," Hannah suggested.

Nate shifted uncomfortably and changed the subject. "How are things going at the Community Center?"

"I guess okay," Becca answered. "I feel horrible though. I'd told the kids we would start doing more hikes, and now I can't lead them. They're going to be so disappointed."

Hannah stole the conversation back. "That's sad, but again, maybe this is God's way of saying that He wants you to spend less time at the Community Center."

"Less time helping people?" Jacic asked.

"Sure. Remember, God is a jealous God. He wants time with you more than anything," Hannah said.

"You think He would hurt me just so I would be so bored out of my mind all I'd do is read my Bible?" Becca asked.

"Well, I don't think He wants you to have that kind of attitude," Hannah responded. "I'm just saying that instead of feeling sorry for yourself, maybe you should try to see why God allowed this to happen."

Tyler squeezed Hannah's arm. "I don't know if Becca's ready to hear this right now," he murmured.

"I don't know if *I'm* ready to hear this right now," Solana said. "Can't *anything* have nothing to do with God?"

"*Everything* has something to do with God. He's the one in complete control," said Hannah.

"Then why does the world seem to be all screwed up?" Solana asked.

Hannah wondered if she was referring less about Becca's leg, and more about Ramón.

"What if God doesn't care?" Solana asked.

"Of course God cares," Hannah argued.

"But what if He doesn't? What if you're all pretending?"

"No. I know God cares," Tyler said. "Sure, crappy things happen. But they happen to everyone."

"I'm with Tyler," Becca said. "Sometimes, like this, I have no idea what God is up to, but I still believe He loves me."

"But why would He?" asked Solana. "I mean, no offense, but there are a lot bigger things going on in the world than whether Tyler gets into his top-choice school."

"But God tells us that He cares for each of us individually. He cares for the birds and the flowers, and even more, He cares for us. He's our Father," Hannah explained.

"Then what kind of father is He? If He's all-powerful, He could have kept Becca from getting hurt, but He didn't. What kind of dad lets their little girl hurt herself without doing anything to stop it?"

No one said anything. Hannah knew God cared, but she couldn't explain it.

"He just does," she sputtered. *Great, what kind of answer is that? He just does?*

"What do you think, Jacie?" Solana continued. "What if God doesn't care?"

Jacie looked down at her shoes. "I've wondered the same thing."

What? Jacie's a believer! What's wrong with my friends?

• • •

Bonfire flames licked at the starry night sky. Hannah loved the warmth from the big fire mixed with the cool October air. It crackled behind her as she surveyed her surroundings, looking for the best photo opportunities. Taking photos at night was difficult, even with the abundance of tiki torches and Japanese lanterns. Colorful leis and grass-skirted students littered the area, drinking pineapple juice out of tiny umbrella-donned plastic glasses. *Click*. A few girls tried to luau dance to the piped-in ukulele music. *Click*. The student council arranged huge pans of barbequed meat on the picnic tables.

"Hannah!" A male voice, coupled with pounding footsteps, called her name.

She turned around. But she already recognized Galvin's voice.

"Hi! How are the pictures going, Miss Photographer?"

"Fine, thank you." His enthusiasm made it difficult to not respond with a smile.

"So you can take a break?"

"Well, I've just started."

"Oh, c'mon, they're doing a limbo contest over there and I know you'd be great at it."

Hannah knew her track record for clumsiness. She'd probably knock herself out trying to limbo.

"Ummm." Hannah thought quickly. "That's probably something that would be great to capture on film. But I don't think I should really—"

"Of course you should! Remember, we're friends. Limbo is the game of friendship." Galvin grabbed her elbow and pulled her toward a crowd of people.

"You just made that up," Hannah laughingly argued, but she let him guide her across the yard.

The game looked easy enough. The others in front of her in line ducked only slightly to avoid hitting the limbo stick.

"Remember you need to lean backward," said one of the stick holders.

"Your turn, Hannah." Galvin nudged her forward.

She bent her knees and waddled up to the stick. Her five-foot, seven-inch frame stood taller than that of most girls her age, and as she looked at the white pole, it seemed much lower than what the other kids had gone under.

She closed her eyes, leaned her head back, and arched her spine. But that threw her bent knees off balance. She wobbled back and forth from one foot to the other before she lost it completely. She fell to the ground to the sound of clapping and laughter.

Kassidy Jordan's voice rang above the crowd. "Well, wasn't that graceful!?"

Hannah opened her eyes to see Galvin's hand extended to help her up.

"I guess it's not my sport," Hannah said. She got herself off the ground, feeling awkward to touch his hand—especially with everyone watching.

"Well, I wouldn't exactly put you on the Olympic limbo team, but I won't hold it against you."

"Thanks," she laughed.

Behind Galvin, she noticed Kassidy watching them. *What am I doing? I'm supposed to be on duty here—taking pictures.* "I better get back to work," she said.

"Okay. Do you need an assistant?"

"Nope." She brushed the grass off her backside. "I work better alone."

A half hour later, Hannah felt like she'd taken enough pictures to capture the mood of the evening. She'd continued to avoid Galvin, who eventually started hanging out with some other guys from their chemistry class. She took a detour into the bathroom before she headed home. Ducking into a stall, she felt the relief of escaping. She felt like she was being watched with critical eyes all evening. She'd have to keep her distance from Galvin to avoid any rumors springing up.

"She'll get my point soon enough."

Hannah's ears perked up. She'd know that voice anywhere. Hannah pulled up her knees so her feet wouldn't be seen.

"She sure got out of that limbo game fast when you shot her a dirty look," another voice laughed. "You really have a vendetta against that poor girl."

"She asked for it," Kassidy said. Hannah heard the clip of Kassidy's lipstick tube. "What do you think of this?"

"Pretty color. Too bright for me, though."

"Perfect for me. Galvin will soon get tired of Miss Sweet-and-Bland and be ready for some excitement. And I'm it. Get outta my way, Hannah Connor."

Hannah held her breath.

The other girl dug through her purse. "He really seems hooked on her, though, doesn't he? I mean, have you ever seen him during class? He just stares at her."

"Well, thanks for making me feel so much better. He'll get bored soon enough. I mean, really, Courtney, have you ever known me to not get the guy I want?"

"True. Kassidy Jordan always gets her man."

"And a prissy slut isn't going to get in my way." Kassidy's voice faded as the two girls headed for the door, but Hannah heard it clearly. "Just watch and see."

The door whispered shut. Hannah exhaled and untwisted her long legs.

She felt a lump in her throat and something else. Anger?

How can she say that about me? What did I ever do to make her hate me so much? Galvin's not her boyfriend, and I'm certainly not trying to steal him. She'd done everything she could tonight to make him leave her alone. *And she's willing to run my name through the mud just because she's jealous? God, if I weren't a Christian, I think I'd slug her.*

She opened the stall door.

Sorry, God. I didn't mean that.

But, deep down, Hannah wasn't really sure that was true.

Anger: *When you're willing to hurt someone even if it means bruising your own fist.*

chapter 11

Hannah got to Becca's later than everyone else the following evening. She'd stayed after school to finish up the layout and hand it over to Aaron—the staff member who'd be taking it to the printer. She'd been pleased with it, beyond what she'd even expected. Each photo told a story, and together the pictures seemed to encapsulate homecoming perfectly. Even Mr. Collins had been impressed.

"Here we are. I'm ready for revenge!" Tyler carried the Trivial Pursuit box over his head as though he were serving an elegant meal.

Solana and Becca relaxed on the couch in the McKinnon basement. Jacie flipped through a magazine, looking at hairstyles. And Hannah slumped on the leather recliner.

"We can't start until Nate gets here so we have even teams," Becca said.

"Do we have to play that game again tonight? It's not

entertaining without a challenge." Solana grinned cockily. "How 'bout we watch a movie instead?"

"How 'bout we give you a handicap then, Miss Know-It-All," said Tyler.

"Yeah," Becca laughed. "We'll put Tyler on your team."

"Hey!" Tyler pounded Becca once with a pillow.

"Be careful. Remember I'm injured."

"Oh, don't give me that. When we're trying to help you by opening the door, you're tough and independent, but when I hit you with a soft pillow, you're suddenly poor, little, vulnerable Becca."

"You're right, I'm sorry. Sit down and I'll give you a back rub."

"Thank you." Tyler hunkered down in front of the couch. "This is the way life should be, surrounded by four beautiful women, a lot of snacks, getting a—YOWZERS!" Tyler leapt to his feet, his back dripping wet.

Becca displayed an innocent smile and set her now-empty glass of ice water on the end table. "I'm sorry. Did I slip?"

"You're in for it!" Tyler said half-laughing, half-shouting. "Just wait until you're off those crutches."

"Watch it, Tyler. Don't drip on my magazine." Jacie held up a picture on the glossy pages. "What do you think of her hair? I could do this to mine."

"For homecoming?" Becca looked doubtful.

"Sure."

"But it's straight. In case you haven't noticed, your hair is anything but," said Solana.

"I know." Jacie ran her fingers through her mass of curls. "But if I use enough straightener and relaxers and blow it dry, it'll go straight."

"I love your hair, though," said Hannah. "I love it curly."

"Yeah, your hair is awesome," said Tyler. "Why do you want to change it?"

"It's just so childish. I feel like it's always poofing up somewhere. I want something more sleek and sophisticated for homecoming."

"But then you wouldn't be Jacie," said Hannah.

"Of course I would. I'll just be the new, improved Jacie."

Tyler reached out for one of Jacie's curls, pulled it taut, and released it to boing back against her cheek. "I don't think it wants to go straight. Besides, you look great with it."

"Ooh, Tyler thinks Jacie looks great," Solana said in her singsongy voice.

Tyler picked at the carpet. "You know what I mean. I just don't think you should change it."

"Maybe not," Jacie said.

"Who's going to escort you at halftime tomorrow?" asked Hannah.

Jacie exchanged a smile with Becca. "Mr. McKinnon," she said.

Becca nodded.

"Becca's dad? That's great," said Hannah. Mr. McKinnon was an obvious choice, really. He'd spent plenty of time around the friends and had been a second father at times for Jacie in the years he'd known her. But Hannah wondered how Becca felt about it.

"Tyler, you should see the dress Jacie's wearing tomorrow. It is HOT!" Solana said.

Jacie's head bobbed up and down with excitement. "I took it home from the shop today. I can't wait to put it on tomorrow."

"You're going to look amazing," Hannah said.

Jacie grinned. "Maybe I'll just wear my hair up," she said.

"With little tendrils hanging down," suggested Solana.

"Hmmm." Jacie piled her hair up on top of her head with a deft twist. "Like this?"

"Yeah, except maybe a little higher."

"And not so tight in the back," Becca added.

"There, perfect," Hannah said.

Tyler leaned against the couch, a bored expression on his face. "Oh, goody. Now tell us what color nail polish you're going to wear!"

"I think silver," said Jacie. "But I'm not sure."

"Oh, no," Tyler groaned. "Please don't start a conversation about this."

"You don't think you want to wear a nice bright red?" Solana asked.

"You're going there," Tyler warned.

"It seems too bold for me, and the silver adds some sparkle."

Tyler raised his voice. "You can come back anytime now. Back to the world of don't give a—"

"I think silver would be really pretty. Especially if your eye shadow had some glitter in it, too," said Becca.

"Good idea," nodded Jacie.

"Just make sure you don't have too much glitter or you'll look like a Christmas ornament," Hannah said.

"Did any of you see the Broncos game Sunday? They had an awesome play in the fourth quarter." He looked around at their blank faces. "Or . . . hey! Listen to this." Tyler straightened and opened his mouth wide, took a deep breath, and—

"NO!" the girls responded in unison.

"Are you going to wear your silver earrings, too?" asked Solana.

"Aauuuugh!" screamed Tyler.

Mrs. McKinnon's voice called from upstairs. "Nate's here, Becca! I'm sending him down."

"Save me, Nate," called Tyler.

"Now can we start the movie?" Solana asked. "Pass the popcorn, Jacie."

Jacie handed her a bowl of popcorn, and then helped herself to a handful of Cool Ranch Doritos.

"Mom got an ice cream cake for later," Becca said. "She thought we might need some cheering up tonight."

"That'll help," Jacie said.

"Hi, everyone." Nate appeared, sauntering down the steps. But he didn't look normal. Was he still upset about Becca being hurt? Becca picked up on it right away, too.

"You okay, Nate?"

He shrugged. Leaning over, he gave Becca a big hug. "I guess I'm just worried about my girl."

Tears pooled in Becca's eyes. "Thanks."

"How can everything go so wrong lately?" Solana asked. "It's like we've got evil leprechauns after us."

"Maybe it's spiritual attack," said Tyler.

"Maybe God's mad at us," suggested Jacie.

"Maybe we're not praying about things enough," said Hannah.

"I prayed about getting into CU Boulder *a lot*," said Tyler.

"And did God really expect us to pray that Becca wouldn't get hurt, and since we didn't, He punished us by making her get hurt?" Jacie sounded irritated with Hannah's suggestion. "That doesn't make sense."

"Well, no." Hannah hadn't meant to offend anyone. "I don't think that just because bad things happen we should blame God."

"But don't you think God could have made the bad things *not* happen?" asked Solana.

"Sure, but sometimes He allows bad things to happen because it's good for us in the long run. Remember, 'All things work together for good for those who love God.' Romans 8:28." *Now what had Dinah said about that verse?*

Solana stood up. "That's crazy. You're saying that God is letting Tyler miss out on his favorite school—the only school he ever wanted to go to. And He's hurting Becca's leg so she can't play basketball. I thought you said God was good!"

"He is. We just can't always understand it." *And I especially don't understand it right now.*

"But how can those things possibly be good things?"

"Well, we know He loves us," Hannah said. But even in her own ears, it felt like a weak argument.

Solana flung her hair back. "Oh, really? Well, *that* kind of love I can do without."

Frustration: *Knowing you have the right answers but getting them lost somewhere in your brain.*

● ● ●

God, I didn't mean to mess things up tonight. Really. I was just trying to stick up for You. I want Solana to believe in You. But, the truth is, I don't know why You are allowing these things to happen. We didn't even mention Kassidy and her friends tonight, but that would be another thing that's gone wrong in what's supposed to be such a "great" senior year. I can't even enjoy going to school, because I'm always watching out for her. Aunt Dinah said You could redeem any situation. I wish I knew how to redeem all these.

Aunt Dinah. That's right. She'd be in Kenya by now. *And I promised to pray for her every day.* She looked at the calendar. *I sure haven't been doing a very good job.* She noticed the lit-up numbers on her clock. 11:00. Suddenly, she realized how tired she was. It had been an emotionally draining day. Her eyes felt heavy. She had to get to school early to help distribute the paper, plus she'd get to see her photo layout in print! *I'll pray tomorrow morning as soon as I get up. I'm just too tired now.*

But you promised, her conscience said in response. Hannah pulled the covers up to her chin. Her pillow sunk under the weight of her head. *Okay, okay . . .*

Dear God, please . . . help . . .

And she drifted off to sleep.

chapter 12

Hannah pumped her bike hard toward the school in the gray of morning. She needed to be there early, but she'd overslept. And by the time she'd finished her morning chores—including getting breakfast for Sarah, Elijah, Daniel, and Rebekah—she'd barely had time to throw on clothes and pull her hair up. She liked to wear her hair down more often these days so it fell like a golden curtain across her back. But today she didn't even have time to comb it. Kassidy and her friends would call it her "librarian do." Of course, so would Solana.

She skidded to a halt in front of the school and rushed to chain her bike to the rack before she hurried inside. A huge "Happy Homecoming" banner waved above the main doors, flapping loudly in the wind. She pulled open the large door.

"It's about time you got here," greeted Brendan, her editor. "I can usually count on you being 10 minutes early—not 10 minutes late."

"Sorry. I overslept," she mumbled. She tried to avoid conversation with Brendan as much as possible, and today was no exception. "What can I do?"

He threw her a string-bound pack of newspapers. "Take these down to the cafeteria. And then help Lydia set up the paper booth outside the office." He plopped a metal cash box on top of the load.

"Can I see one first?" Of course she'd seen the layout before it had been taken to the printer yesterday, but she was anxious to see how it turned out on the printed page.

"Later. We've got too much to do."

He was right. By the time Hannah had stopped off at the cafeteria, there was already a line of early-bird students waiting to purchase a paper. And the rush continued up through the first bell. Hannah had permission to get to her first-hour class a few minutes late on Friday, but Lydia had to run.

"See you later!" she shouted back to Hannah.

Hannah began to close up the cash box and collect the disarrayed newspapers. *Maybe now I can see the layout.*

"Can I get a paper, please?" a voice asked.

"Sure." Hannah grabbed the top copy off her now-organized pile. "Here you go."

Kassidy grinned at her.

"Oh. Hi, Kassidy."

"Your photo layout is the talk of the school," Kassidy said, dropping her change into Hannah's open palm.

That's strangely sweet of her. "Thanks," Hannah said. "I haven't had a chance to see it yet."

"You'll have to take a look," Kassidy said. She raised one eyebrow and gave Hannah a half grin. Then she spun on her heels and left.

How odd, Hannah thought. She felt a shiver and chased it away. Still, she quickly grabbed a paper off the stack. Before she opened it she checked the staff box at the bottom of page one. There it was: "Photographer: Hannah Connor," and below it "Layout Designer: Hannah Connor." *Perfect. They remembered.* The second bell rang.

"Miss Connor," a voice interrupted.

"Oh, hi, Mr. Shaw."

"I'm aware you have special permission to be tardy on paper day, but I don't think you should take advantage of it."

"I'm sorry?"

"This isn't time for you to sit back and read the paper, it's time to allow you to return the cash box to the journalism lab and get to class as quickly as possible."

"Oh." Yikes, he must be watching her like a hawk. "I'm sorry. I'll go now." She picked up the stack of papers and balanced the cash box on top.

"Good idea. Have a nice day, Hannah."

"Thank you, sir." She headed down the hall.

"Oh, and Hannah?" Mr. Shaw called.

Hannah turned around. "Yes, sir?"

"Nice job on the photo layout. It's always one of my favorite features of the homecoming paper."

The principal even noticed! And he knew that she was the one who put it together! "Thank you, Mr. Shaw."

Even Kassidy had complimented her on the page today. Hannah hummed her way to the journalism lab. Although the morning had started out on the wrong foot, it looked like it would be a great day after all.

Streamers and balloons filled the hallways, making Hannah feel like she was walking inside a huge blue-and-white cake. Posters encouraging the Stallions to pummel the Cougars hung at every corner. She could feel the electricity in the air. And she was a part of it.

She eased silently into her English class where Mr. Garner

was discussing the various patterns of story plots. Hannah opened her English text in front of her and then unfolded the paper in her lap. She'd take a quick peek and then concentrate on Mr. Garner's lecture. She breathed out a sigh as she opened up to the center. The colors had turned out even better than she'd imagined. And it looked balanced. *Wait a minute, this looks different . . . oh no!* She gasped audibly.

Mr. Garner stopped mid-lecture. "Are you okay, Hannah?"

Hannah nodded, quickly folding up the newspaper and throwing it into her backpack, as though she could keep anyone else from seeing it. But she knew she couldn't. Already hundreds of kids had looked at the collage—had looked at that picture. Even the principal had seen it. What must he think?

She closed her eyes, trying to make the picture go away. But she couldn't. Imprinted in her mind was that photo. A close-up of Hannah Connor's face just inches away from Galvin Parker's, looking as if they were about to kiss.

Who took this? When? Where? She and Galvin had never been ready to kiss. EVER.

Hundreds of kids. Maybe everyone had seen it. What did *they* think about her now?

Humiliation: *When the intensity with which you want to disappear matches the intensity of the redness on your face.*

● ● ●

A sea of blue-and-white-clad students poured through the hallways—more hyperactive than on most Fridays. The promise of shortened classes and an extended afternoon pep rally added to the excitement.

But Hannah was only looking for two people. She always saw Jacie and Tyler on their way between classes. *There they are.*

It wasn't hard to see them. Tyler was wearing a suit and tie today, as he was escorting Jacie at the pep rally that afternoon. She waved them down.

"Hannah, great spread," said Jacie. She looked pretty in her black skirt and powder blue sweater, Hannah noticed. "But I was surprised to—"

"What was with that picture of you and Galvin?" Tyler jutted in. "It looks like you're about to liplock!"

"Tyler!" Jacie chastised him. "I mean, it did kind of look like that, but it's still the best homecoming spread I've seen."

"Yeah," Tyler agreed. "That's the only page I've seen open today. Everyone's looking at it."

"You don't get it." Hannah had to raise her voice to be heard. "I didn't put that picture in there!"

"You didn't? Then how—"

"I don't know," Hannah whined. "Someone must have stuck it in there after I left yesterday. I don't know." She heard her own voice crack and willed herself not to cry. "I don't even know when it was taken. I've never seen it before."

"How weird. Who would put that in there?" Jacie said.

Hannah shook her head. The only person who came to mind was Kassidy—*but how could she pull that off?*

"Hey, Hannah!" Galvin's voice rose from behind Hannah's shoulder. "I liked your pictures."

"Thanks," Hannah mumbled, avoiding his eyes. She didn't want anyone seeing her look at him—ever again. What must the student body think? And her teachers? And parents would buy the papers tonight at the game. *Everyone will think I want to be with Galvin.*

Galvin seemed oblivious to her discomfort. "I didn't even know someone was taking our picture during the limbo contest."

The limbo contest. Of course. Someone had taken a shot right when Galvin helped her up off the ground. But who would be watching that closely to get a close-up like that? *Kassidy hadn't had a camera*, Hannah remembered. *But one of her friends might have*.

"Well, I gotta go." Galvin excused himself. "See you in chemistry, Hannah."

● ● ●

Chemistry class was miserable. Of course, the whole day had been miserable. Instead of walking in the limelight, Hannah spent the day trying to make herself invisible. Who knew what people were thinking about her? She could hear them saying, "Yeah, I guess Hannah the photographer thinks homecoming is about school spirit, a football game, and making out."

She sat slumped over her desk as Dr. Hanson peered over the rims of his blue glasses, gazing from one student to another. Thankfully, it was a test day so she didn't have to interact with anyone. But she could still hear the giggles and feel the stares from Kassidy's corner. Galvin tried to get her attention on her way in, but Hannah made sure not to meet his eyes. She wasn't going to encourage him in any way. Barely able to concentrate on the test in front of her, she filled in the multiple-choice answers.

The more she thought about the day, the more angry she became. She'd worked hard on that photo spread. How dare someone come in and alter it with a photo that had nothing to do with homecoming. How dare someone try to slam her reputation. *No, it's not someone. It's Kassidy*. And she'd get to the bottom of it yet.

Hannah brought her finished test up to the front and laid it on top of the pile. Dr. Hanson held a copy of the *Stony Brook High Times*, reading it intently. *Great, he'll see it, too. Everyone will think Galvin and I are going out*. She returned to her seat and fiddled with her pencil. She'd have to talk to Galvin about it, too. *After I made it so clear I wasn't interested in him. He probably thinks I'm playing hard to get. First, flirting with him. Then acting cold. And now posting a picture of us in the center of the newspaper.* She'd been too frustrated to explain the situation to him earlier that day, but maybe she could catch him after class. She fiddled more with her pencil.

Dr. Hanson pushed up his glasses as the bell rang. "That will be all for today. Please make sure you—"

Hannah couldn't hear the rest of his sentence over the herd of students stampeding out the classroom door.

She gathered her things. Galvin waited next to her.

"It was a mistake," she said before he could say anything. "The picture of us wasn't supposed to have gone in the photo spread. I hadn't even seen it before."

"Oh, c'mon, Hannah. Don't give me that." He followed her to the door. "I hate all the mixed signals. Be up front with me."

She turned to look at him. She didn't want to be rude. She hadn't meant to hurt him. How could she explain this?

Apparently, her face said it best. "You're serious," he said. "You didn't put it in there."

"Someone took the picture at the luau and replaced it with another photo after I left last night. I promise. I couldn't have been more surprised to see it there this morning."

Galvin nodded. "But who would do that?"

"I have my ideas, but I don't want to say anything."

"But why would someone do it? To be funny? To have Miss Prude making eyes with the New Kid? Is that what entertains people?"

Miss Prude? Is that what he thinks of me? "What did you just call me?"

Galvin immediately looked apologetic. "I'm sorry. Really. I just heard someone else call you that the other day." He paused. "You know I like you, Hannah. I wouldn't call you that."

"Who said that about me?" she asked.

"Kassidy Jordan."

Hannah nodded. *Wow. What a surprise.*

"Who do you think replaced the picture?"

"You just answered your own question."

● ● ●

"So did you have a nice little chat with Galvin?" asked Kassidy from behind her. "How does he feel about his new-found fame?"

Does that girl just follow me around all day looking for question-able things I do?

Hannah turned to face her. "Hi, Kassidy," she said, sounding worn out even to herself. *God, help me be kind. Or at least not slug her.*

"I guess you're not trying too hard to hide your interest now. Shoot, you're publishing your desires," Kassidy said.

"I didn't put that photo in the newspaper," said Hannah, her jaw set.

"You can deny it all you want, Hannah. But the proof is in the picture. You want Galvin Parker, and now the whole school knows it."

Hannah bit the inside of her cheek. She needed to know if Kassidy was the one behind the scheme, or if there was someone else out there—someone on the newspaper staff—who had it in for her. Kassidy certainly didn't seem to be hiding anything.

"Did you—did you somehow get the picture in there?" Hannah asked her.

"Oh, please. If you're going to publicize your crushes, at least be big enough to admit them." Kassidy acted nonchalantly enough, but Hannah could see her forehead twitch slightly. "Especially considering you're not as holy as we all thought."

chapter 13

When Hannah approached the lunch table, carrying her salad and burger, Solana was already there with the newspaper spread out in front of her.

"I have to admit," Solana said, her eyes cool as she glanced toward Hannah, "I expected some competition from Kassidy. But having you in the picture is a surprise."

Oh, no. Not her, too. How am I going to explain this? She didn't care—at least too much—what Kassidy thought of her. But this was her friend—a friend she hadn't been entirely honest with.

"I'm not interested in him, Solana," Hannah protested, dropping her plate with a clatter on the other side of the table. She felt annoyed that she sounded so defensive. She hadn't done anything wrong. "Galvin asked me to be his lab partner. I agreed, thinking that if I did things your way he would leave me alone." She hoped that at least Solana would hear her. "Obviously it didn't work. Besides, Sol, he's not interested in you."

"Like you ever gave him the chance." Solana folded her arms and tossed her hair off her shoulder. "You've been too busy entertaining him yourself."

"It was your idea to keep your distance and play hard-to-get. Unfortunately I happened to always be in his way."

"But I didn't keep my distance so you could go in for the kill," Solana said.

For the kill? This was all a game to Solana. And Galvin wasn't the prize; he was just the last box on the CANDY LAND path. "Why do you care so much?" Hannah heard her voice rise an octave and tried to calm herself. "I mean, it's not even as though you really like Galvin. You're still in love with Ramón. You just want to use Galvin to prove something to yourself . . . and forget who you *really* care about."

Solana's cool air was broken for a minute, as though shocked that someone could see straight through her. "I do like Galvin. Sure, he doesn't even come close to Ramón, but even you thought it was a good idea to start dating again."

"Only because I know Ramón isn't good for you."

"How can you say that?"

"He's not a believer," Hannah said.

"Hello. Earth to Hannah. Neither am I."

Hannah couldn't say how she felt. She didn't want Solana to be happy with a nonbeliever, because then she'd never learn to need God. She'd just go along and enjoy life and not see where it was lacking. At least in this place—without Ramón—she knew something was keeping her from feeling joy, even if she still wouldn't admit it was God. "*And* he caused you to make some stupid mistakes."

"He didn't *cause* the mistakes. Having sex with him was *my* choice. It was *my* fault," Solana argued.

"Well, he certainly didn't try to talk you out of it," Hannah mumbled.

Jacie and Tyler approached, laughing about something that happened in the lunch line. Nate and Becca were behind them. Nate balanced two lunch trays while Becca struggled with her crutches.

Tyler noticed the serious tone of the table conversation. "Well, what are we discussing here?"

"Ramón," said Solana. "And Galvin."

"Oh, yeah. How's the experiment going?" asked Jacie. Hannah noticed her cheeks looked a little pinker than normal. *She must be excited about being in homecoming court.*

"It would be going much better, if some people weren't trying to get in the way." She tapped the photo of Hannah and Galvin with a long, brightly painted fingernail.

"I never put the picture in there," Hannah said.

"I know, I know. Jacie told Becca, who told me last hour, but that doesn't make the picture any less true. Anyone looking at this could tell you both have an interest in each other. And that's fine, Hannah. But at least be up front with me about it."

Hannah exhaled in frustration. "I admit, I didn't tell you that he was interested in me because I didn't want to hurt your feelings. But I don't like him, I—"

"I don't really want to hear this right now. If you'll all excuse me, I think I'm going to go to the library for lunch." Solana stood up and marched out of the lunchroom, her heeled boots clicking her irritation on the linoleum floor.

"Whoa," Tyler said. "It's been a while since I've seen her that upset."

Nate, Becca, Tyler, and Jacie watched for Hannah's reaction.

"I didn't mean to make her angry," Hannah mumbled into her salad. She knew she'd hit a nerve in Solana's pride. Solana hated to be "protected" from getting her feelings hurt. She always preferred honesty to sympathy. *I really blew that one. Seems like she should be getting used to me messing things up by now.*

"Should one of us go talk to her?" asked Jacie.

"I think Solana wants to be alone," said Becca. "Don't feel this is all you, Hannah. She's been missing Ramón like crazy. We were talking about it earlier today and she was practically in tears."

"Poor Solana," Jacie said.

Hannah nodded. She felt some guilt quivering in her stomach when she thought about the things she'd said about Ramón. *No wonder she got so angry.*

"It might be in your best interest, Hannah, if you keep your distance from Galvin for a while," Tyler said.

Something in the tone of his voice made Hannah think Tyler was talking about more than the Solana situation. Most likely, he'd heard Kassidy or one of her friends spreading rumors. But she didn't ask him about it. Some things were better left alone.

● ● ●

Sparks of light from the last of the halftime fireworks show made their way earthward, leaving a trail of fluorescent color behind. The band broke into the school song, and everyone jumped to their feet to clap. Hannah could smell the mustard from Tyler's hot dog. She loved this—cuddled up in a wool blanket on a crisp night. She loved the excitement of the crowd and the lights illuminating the football field. The only awkward aspect was the remaining tension between her and Solana.

Becca squeezed her shoulder. "Jacie's up next," she said.

"Yeah, Jacie!" called Tyler, letting out a piercing whistle.

The announcer came on mic. "And now for this year's homecoming court! The lovely ladies were driven around the track this evening in vehicles donated by Eastbank Chevrolet. Our first nominee, stepping out of the red Corvette, is Jacie Noland!"

Hannah's grin barely fit her face, watching Jacie walk across the football field in her beautiful blue gown. The announcer followed the script perfectly. "Jacie Noland, escorted by family friend Ted McKinnon, plans to study art. Jacie's activities include Art Club, leadership at The Edge, community volunteer projects, and working at Raggs by Razz. Jacie's dress this evening is being provided by Raggs by Razz."

Jacie looked perfect. Her eyes glowed. Her feet seemed light walking across the football field, although Hannah knew her pointed heels must be sinking into the soft ground.

"She looks amazing," said Becca.

Nate, Tyler, Hannah, and Solana agreed. The four of them cheered as loudly as they could, and Hannah clicked off a few photos, not for the paper, just for her. She and Solana sat side by side, with an unspoken peace treaty between them for the time being. They wouldn't let differences get in the way on Jacie's night. Hannah had whispered a quick apology after the first quarter, and Solana returned with one of her own, but they both knew it wasn't completely settled.

The announcer then introduced the other candidates: Jessica Abbott and Kassidy Jordan. Through her telephoto lens, Hannah saw Jacie's face twitch nervously. But it was only because she knew Jacie so well that she could tell. Anyone else would say she wore a perfect smile the entire time. Kassidy promenaded onto the field, wearing a dress that left little to the imagination. Mermaid style, it clung to every curve, with a slit high on her thigh and a plunging neckline.

"Dynamite dress," Solana said.

Catcalls came from all across the stands. *How could her dad walk right next to her and let her wear that kind of dress?* She knew her own dad would be covering up her chest with his suit coat if she ever wore a dress like that.

Uh, oh. She noticed Galvin heading up the steps toward the group. He looked decidedly cute in his Stallions baseball cap and leather jacket, but she didn't dwell on it. *Distance, distance, distance,* she reminded herself.

By now, Galvin was excusing himself past a row of knees to get to the group, and Solana had noticed him as well. She raised her eyebrows at Hannah. "Are you going to give me a chance?" she whispered. Hannah nodded, leaving her eyes fixed on the field.

Galvin sat down next to her, but she pretended not to notice.

"And this year's homecoming queen is—" the announcer echoed from the speakers. A drum roll tattered from the percussion pit.

"C'mon, Jacie!" shouted Tyler.

"Not Kassidy," Hannah prayed out loud.

"Jessica Abbott!" the announcer shouted.

Cheers erupted from the stands, and even Hannah gave a few halfhearted claps. No one in the group—except occasionally Tyler—was a huge fan of Jessica, but anyone was better than Kassidy.

Jacie, down on the field, clapped politely and gave Jessica a hug. Kassidy stood with a stone-faced smile, as if in disbelief.

"You think Jacie is disappointed?" asked Galvin.

Solana took advantage of Hannah's silence. "Not really. She thought making court was a fluke. She never expected to be crowned queen. She just felt honored that she was nominated."

"So what do you think of the game so far?" Galvin said. It was kind of an odd thing to ask since the Stony Brook Stallions were getting stomped to pieces: 21-0 at halftime.

Tyler laughed. "Well, the halftime show has been good."

Hannah thought about excusing herself to get a drink, but then Galvin might volunteer to come along. *Better to just sit here and act like a dunce.*

"Galvin," Solana said, leaning over Hannah to put her hand

on Galvin's knee. "You know a lot about football. Maybe you could explain it to me. These people aren't any help."

Oh, please, thought Hannah. Solana probably knew more about football than Galvin—she was always explaining it to everyone else. *I guess she gave up on the experiment.*

Galvin seemed uncomfortable. "Uh, what do you want to know?"

"I can barely hear you," said Solana. "Here, let me switch places with Hannah."

"But Hannah might want to know what's going on, too. And I can explain it to both of you. Why don't I sit in the middle?"

"You don't really care about football, though. Do you, Hannah?" Solana asked, politely enough under the glare.

"Nope." At least she could be honest. "Y'know, I think I'm going to go down and find Jacie. I'll be right back." Hannah stood up to make her escape.

"Oh, I'll come with you," Galvin volunteered.

"I thought you were explaining football to Solana," Hannah said.

"Well, if he doesn't want to—" Solana sounded almost sulky.

Becca's phone rang. "Hello?" She paused while listening. "Hi, Mrs. Connor. Yeah, she's right here."

Hannah's parents never called her on her friends' phones while she was out. There was never a reason to. Hannah was very conscious about getting home on time and keeping her parents informed of her whereabouts. Part of her felt relieved to be rescued from this terribly awkward conversation, but the other part felt concerned. *Why would they be calling?* Had they seen the picture of her and Galvin? Were they upset with her? She couldn't believe she hadn't even thought about how her parents would react.

"Okay, I'll tell her." Becca hung up the phone.

"What did they say?" Hannah asked.

"They want you to come home right now."

● ● ●

Hannah rehearsed her explanation as she took her time trudging up the front steps. Moths flitted around the porch lamp, casting shadows in the warm light. She took a deep breath. *Mom, Dad, I know it's hard to believe, but Galvin was only helping me up when I fell down. I didn't know someone took the picture, and I don't know how it got into the newspaper.* She bit her lip. Even to her it sounded implausible.

She opened the door and saw her parents sitting side by side on the couch. *Uh oh, this was serious.* Mom even had a box of Kleenex next to her, as though news of Hannah's indiscretion had brought her to tears. Hannah knew her parents thought of her as the "good kid"—the one who wouldn't give them any trouble. She hated disappointing them. Already, today had made Hannah Connor's top 10 list of bad days. Could it get any worse?

Her parents looked up as she closed the door behind her.

Hannah swallowed, her throat instantly dry. "Hi. I came home as soon as I could."

Dad looked at Mom. Mom took a deep breath. She clutched a wadded Kleenex. "Hannah, have a seat."

Hannah stumbled into a chair and clasped her hands on her lap. She'd be strong. Once her parents knew what really happened, they'd understand. She was certain of it—almost.

Dad cleared his throat. "We received a call from your Uncle Greg a little while ago."

Uncle Greg? "Why?" Hannah's heart took off in a sprint.

"There was a train accident on their way to Mombasa."

An accident?

Her dad swallowed. "Hannah." Dad paused. "Dinah was killed."

chapter 14

Her mom began to sob, but it sounded like it was coming from another part of the house—or maybe outside. A humming rang in her ears that blocked everything else out.

"Bridge collapsed." "Train cars fell." "Died instantly." Her dad's words echoed as though shouted from the top of the Grand Canyon. But she kept hearing "Dinah was killed. Dinah was killed. Dinah—"

"That's ridiculous," she smiled.

Her mom's eyes widened.

"It's Kenya. Probably some Kenyan terrorist's idea of a joke. They're just saying that. It's Kenya." *Of course. Aunt Dinah was fine.*

Mrs. Connor reached for Hannah's shoulder. "Greg called us, honey. He told us himself." Her mother's gentle touch annoyed her and she shrugged it off.

This wasn't true. This couldn't be true. It was a lie. A total and complete lie.

Hannah jumped up. "Well, they tricked him. She's not dead. I know she's not dead!"

"Hannah—" her dad began.

She turned and bolted up the stairs. "It's not true!" she yelled back as she clambered up the steps. Not her aunt with the perky smile, and the wonderful life, and the little one growing inside of her. She shouted from the top, "She's having a baby. She's having McKenzie!"

Of course, she's not dead. She was on a missions trip. God didn't let people die on missions trips. God didn't let people die who were on their way to help other people—to even save lives. God didn't let people die who were going to have babies. God didn't do things like this. God sent miraculous recoveries and gave wonderful surprises. Remember? Aunt Dinah had said that herself. *Good things are yet to come*, she'd told Hannah as she left that previous Sunday. She told Hannah that so Hannah wouldn't lose hope, so she would know the truth.

Hannah didn't know how long she lay on her bed facedown. Her pillow was damp when the door opened. "Hannah . . ." her mom's voice said.

"It's not true," Hannah said flatly.

"It's hard for all of us, honey."

Hannah spun around to face her mother, and all her emotion raged out in a blinding scream. "IIT'S . . . NOOOT . . . TRUUUE!" Her throat rattled and the sound terrified her as much as the look on her mom's face.

Her mother burst into fitful tears and rushed to wrap her arms around Hannah's stiffened body. "I'm sorry, sweetie," she choked. Her flooded eyes stared into Hannah's. "It *is* true."

Hannah choked and gasped. The pain was drowning her. She collapsed into her mom's arms, her body convulsing with sobs. "No . . . no . . . no . . ." She wanted to push her mom away, but found herself hiding in her lap, her face pressed against her starched skirt.

Oh, God, how could You do this?

● ● ●

"Your mom called," Becca explained when Hannah entered the living room filled with her friends.

Hannah looked from one friend to another. Jacie was blotting her eyes with a Kleenex. Becca's face was red and swollen from crying. Solana bit one side of her cheek and then the other, looking around the room as if she could find something to say. Tyler sat leaning forward, his elbows on his knees and hands clasped, as though he were about to say something meaningful and poignant but couldn't remember what it was.

"We're so sorry," Jacie said.

The others nodded.

"Is there anything we can do?" Becca asked.

The others nodded.

Hannah shook her head.

"Are you okay?" Tyler asked.

"I don't know. I don't even want to think about it. I can't believe it happened. She's . . . gone."

Hannah's face remained dry. She felt her tears had run dry, and yet they seemed to be welling in the pit of her stomach and into her chest. "I don't understand how it could happen. It doesn't make sense. She was only helping people."

The others nodded.

"She was pregnant with a precious life. She was there to do missionary work. She was wonderful. Why would God allow this to happen?"

The others shook their heads. Jacie bit the back of her hand, her eyes wide and frightened.

Hannah thought she should say something to make it better—to make her friends feel less awkward and make her heart ache a little less. *She's in a better place*, she thought she should say. But the words made her want to scream and hit something. The words might be technically true, but Hannah hated them. She wanted Dinah *here*!

Jacie smoothed the front of the sheer blue dress she was wearing. She still looked beautiful.

"Jacie, it's homecoming. You should be at the dance." She looked at all her friends. "You should all go. I'll be fine."

"We're not going anywhere," said Becca. "Just let us be your friends."

Just be a friend, Dinah had said.

How did she keep showing up?

● ● ●

Hannah woke up Saturday morning, wondering why her body felt stiff and her face heavy. It only took her a second to remember. *Aunt Dinah*. Had it all been a dream? She remembered her friends gathered around her last night, talking and crying until midnight. She couldn't recall what they'd talked about, but she remembered them being there. Jacie in her blue silk dress. Yes, it really happened.

Numbness enveloped her the rest of the day. She went through the motions of normal life. She bathed the twins. She stroked Rebekah's hair as the younger girl cried. But her own emotions felt distant—as though Rebekah's sadness was because Daniel had ruined her favorite homemade necklace, not because Aunt Dinah was never coming back.

She made sandwiches for everyone at lunchtime. She did laundry. She felt the weight on the house, like the air was heavy with grief. All of her friends called at some point during the day, asking if she wanted to hang out, asking if she'd like for them to come over, asking if there was anything they could do. But she just wanted to be with her family today.

The twins still didn't really understand. They'd never known anyone who died before. Except Jesus. Did they think Aunt Dinah would be resurrected in three days?

I wish she would.

Every time Hannah closed her eyes to remember her aunt, she looked so alive—so vibrant. Like she'd always seen her.

Like she'd always been.

She'd tried that day to be productive, to be helpful, but nothing seemed to have a point. And how could she throw all her energy into something that—in the whole scheme of life—mattered for nothing? And that's the category everything fit into—cleaning the house, doing homework, watching TV.

Mom made hot dogs for dinner—no buns—and served them with a carton of cottage cheese. As odd as it was for Mrs. Connor to fix anything but a wholesome meal including all four food groups, it had been just as odd that no one commented on the "meal" she served. Hardly anyone touched their food. Already a stack of foil-covered casserole dishes filled the fridge. It seemed like all the "we're so sorry" church people had rung the doorbell that day.

"Oh, Gretchen. I'm so sorry. Here's a little something. Let me know if there's anything we can do," they'd cluck in their maternal voices.

Hannah's mom always smiled and murmured a kind thank-you, but her eyes remained blank. "How kind. It smells lovely."

The new casserole was added to the pile.

Hot dogs with cottage cheese were served for dinner.

And no one noticed.

A knock came on her bedroom door.

"Come in," Hannah said.

The door swung open to reveal Rebekah, wearing her little

pink sweatsuit. It was her comfort-wear, the thing she wore when she felt sick or for an entire week after Mr. and Mrs. Connor broke the news that the family would be moving, and for days when Flea-Fi, the family cat, died. The legs were getting too short, and the cuffs on the sleeves had worn into frayed masses. Hannah knew she'd be seeing the outfit a lot in the near future.

"Hi," Rebekah said. She looked much younger than 11. She looked around Hannah's room, back at Hannah, and then at the floor.

"Do you want to come and sit with me for a while?" Hannah asked.

Rebekah nodded and scampered up onto the bed and into Hannah's arms. Hannah held the little girl tight and brushed clumps of sticky hair away from her face.

They sat that way for a long time, Rebekah tucked under Hannah's protective arm, leaning against her chest.

"Why?" the little girl squeaked out finally.

Even though silent tears ran down her cheeks, Hannah pretended she was asleep.

● ● ●

That evening, she opened her Bible to read, as usual. But the words were just black lines on white paper. She remembered her promise to pray for Dinah. *I never did,* she thought. *What would have been different if I'd prayed? Would she have lived?* She read through her journal and found the last entry. The pen hung listlessly in her hand, but no words would come. She couldn't write. She didn't want to write. What was the point? She was mad at herself for not praying like she was supposed to. Was God punishing her? And what kind of God would kill a woman who only wanted to serve Him, a woman who was carrying a *baby*? What kind of God would do that?

"She was only trying to serve You," she whispered into the air. Tears slipped down her face. If they kept on, her cheeks would have crevices carved in them. Grand Canyon cheeks.

If God didn't care about Dinah, then who did He care about? Certainly not her. What was she doing spending her entire life trying to please Him? Why did it matter where she went to school or who she witnessed to? What did anything matter?

A yellow steno pad sat opened on her dresser. *McKenzie's Shower* it said at the top. Printed underneath were the words *yellow ducks*. She remembered the ideas that had flowed as she wrote down those words. Cute little duck invitations that could be opened by lifting a yellow wing. A giant fluffy yellow cake in the shape of a duck. A big banner saying, "Congratulations!"

Why?! She opened her mouth to scream the words but nothing came out past the blockage of a waiting sob. *Why? Why? Why? Why? Why? How could You do this, God? And I trusted You! I really trusted You!*

She flung the pen across the room, leaving a black mark on the wall when it thunked against it. She didn't care. She put her face into the pillow and sobbed so hard it ripped inside her chest.

Sleep didn't come easy that night. Despite all her efforts, her busyness that day hadn't brought her to the point of exhaustion. Lying on her bed, she could see the stars outside her window. Dried branches scratched against the glass where, only a couple weeks ago, green leaves had fluttered—so alive.

In all this restlessness, she'd try the one place where she always found peace. She grabbed a winter coat from a hook, pulled on a knit cap, and creaked open the window out to the roof. She crawled onto the black shingles, cautiously attempting to make as little noise as possible.

Pulling her knees up to her chin, she wrapped her arms

around her legs. The stars were clear in the cold night air. Already her nose felt numb. She swiped at her runny nose with the back of her hand. She peered through overhanging branches to search for the star Aunt Dinah had given her. There it was. Owen, the star that told her God was there. How dare that star shine his face tonight? How could God be there?

Grief: *When your heart turns inside out and all the contents empty into your stomach and throat.*

"God, how could You do this?" she whispered into the empty air, leaving a white cloud of frozen breath. "Why would You do this? It doesn't make sense. Why don't You care?"

Headlights pulled into the driveway. *Who would be visiting now?* she thought. *It must be after two.* The headlights switched off. A car door slammed. A figure made his way toward the door. Hannah recognized the lanky build even though he walked more slumped than usual. It was Uncle Greg.

She crawled back through the window, took off her coat and hat, and padded down the stairs to hear what was going on.

She squatted at the top of the stairs to listen and watch. Greg was still hugging her mom. Mr. Connor awkwardly patted Greg's shoulder.

"Sit down, Greg," Mrs. Connor said. "I'll get you some tea."

Greg sat on the edge of the couch as if ready to flee at any moment. Mr. Connor sat across from him in his easy chair. He handed Greg a box of tissues. Hannah couldn't see Greg's face but guessed that he was either crying or on the verge of tears. Her dad had streams running down his own face.

"I still can't believe Dinah's . . . ." Greg choked. "Gone," he said in a very small voice.

Mr. Connor nodded, swallowing hard.

"It's so unreal. I keep hoping I'll wake up to her laughing."

"When did you get in?" Mr. Connor asked. "Why didn't you call? We would have come to get you."

"We landed a couple of hours ago." Greg put his hand up and waved off his concerns. "I didn't want to bother you. Pastor Roy and Vickie came to the airport to pick up the high school kids in church vans. Some of the parents were there, too. Once I was sure everyone knew which carousel the luggage would arrive on, I went looking for Dinah." His voice shook. "Can you believe it? At first I casually look around, expecting her to emerge from the ladies' room. And then, when she doesn't appear, I start looking from face to face, looking frantically for her. *Where is she?* And then I remembered."

Hannah wondered why her father didn't interrupt. Greg just paused and continued to ramble. "I get the luggage. Hers, too. I find the car. I must've said good-bye to people. I don't remember. And the car feels so empty. It still smells like her. I passed the exit on the way here, like I always do, and I could hear her say, 'Uh, Greg, you did it again.'" Greg stopped talking and Hannah could see his shoulders shake. "I loved her so much." He put his head into his hands and sobbed.

"I know," Mr. Connor said, "I know." He leaned forward, sat back, leaned forward again like he might get up. His face twisted with not knowing what to do.

Mrs. Connor entered, carrying a tray of teacups. She set them down on the coffee table, sat on the couch next to Greg, and put her arm around his shoulders. She spoke indecipherable words of comfort.

Greg took a deep breath and sat up. Mrs. Connor handed him a cup of tea. He stared at it as if he didn't know what to do with it. His large hands turned the dainty cup around and around.

Mrs. Connor touched his arm. "Do you want to tell us what happened?"

He nodded. He started talking, in a softer voice than Hannah could make out. She silently slipped down the stairs, one step at a time, to be able to hear.

"It replays over and over again in my mind. I suppose I keep hoping the ending will be different."

He looked up at Hannah's parents, turning his head first to one, then the other. "She comes to me from where she'd been sitting talking with a group of her girls. I hear her say, 'Greg, I'm going to get some water, do you want anything?' I was reading a magazine and just shook my head. I didn't even look up." His voice quivered. He took a quick gulp of hot tea and continued.

"Why didn't I get up to get the water for her? Why couldn't I have done that?"

"It's okay," Mrs. Connor said. "You've always loved and served Dinah. I bet she didn't think twice about it."

Greg turned his head to look long and hard at Mrs. Connor.

"Then?" Mr. Connor said gently. Hannah guessed he really wanted to know what happened to his baby sister—wanted and didn't want to know at the same time. *Why is it that our curiosity is stronger than not wanting to hear something horrible?* she wondered.

"She squeezed my shoulder. I looked up and she gave me a brilliant smile. I touched her hand and smiled back. I returned to reading my magazine. In that moment I noticed, just barely, the train was crossing a bridge. A few moments later—maybe a minute or two—a loud crack with a deafening groaning of wood brought me out of my reading. The whole train began to shake and shimmy. It jolted backwards, throwing everything forward for a split second. People screamed. I looked back for Dinah."

Greg's hands shook. He dropped the teacup back on its saucer. "I heard . . . I heard . . . from words passing from person to person that—a car was off the track, dangling over the ravine, and then . . . then dropping."

No one said anything. The clock ticked. Hannah strained forward.

Greg took another deep breath and started talking fast. "I raced to the side of the train. I couldn't see anything. They were making all these announcements over the intercom. A couple of the kids had cuts. All of them were crying. One looked like he had a broken arm. I moved past them to look out the rear window—the door leading to the car behind us. Between the couplings I could barely see two cars in the ravine. I could even see tiny bodies of people lying there. But I didn't see Dinah. It was too far down."

He buried his face in his hands for a minute. Mr. and Mrs. Connor waited, both wiping away silent tears. Hannah noticed, for the first time, the wet spots on her knees from where tears had soaked into her pajama bottoms. Greg yanked two tissues from the box and blew. He crumpled them and dropped them on the table with a growing herd of others. Like crumpled sheep gathering. Hannah stared at them, growing evidence of the truth: *Dinah really is dead.*

Oh, God.

"People. Official-looking people evacuated the train and had us walk along the track to wait for vehicles from local villages to come. Jeeps. Trucks. They planned to shuttle us to the hospital. I had to stay with the kids. I had to look for Dinah. I looked everywhere for the green sweater—the one Hannah bought her. Dinah had said she was too cold." He let out a choked laugh. "So much like Dinah. We're practically on the equator and she's still cold.

"I asked one of the sponsors to stay with the kids. I needed to find Dinah. I knew she had to be alive. She'd been marched out of the car with the rest of the passengers and I'd find her in the crowd. I *had* to find her. I called her name over and over and over.

"When I got closer to the ravine, I couldn't see anything. It was all smoke and darkness. But I searched every face that hiked up the sides. I ignored the people who had come to help. They didn't want me to go down there. I told them I needed to find my wife. I slid down the sides, passing people being carried up on makeshift stretchers. The alive ones moaned something horrible. Some screamed when the stretchers jostled. By then, I was so scared. I began to pray so hard that I'd hear Dinah scream. At least then I'd know she was alive. And then . . ." His voice broke. The remaining words came out in a loud whisper. "And then came a guy carrying a limp woman. She wore a . . . green . . . sweater. I reached out to the man and took her from him. I cradled her in my arms. 'Oh, sweetie. Oh, my girl. I love you, Dinah. You're going to be okay.' But the man stared at me. 'I'm sorry, sir. She's dead.'" His voice cracked and he stopped for a minute.

He was there. Right there. Why didn't he go to her sooner? Hannah wanted to scream.

And then, as unexpectedly to her as to the others oblivious to her presence, the words erupted. "Why didn't you look for her sooner? You could have done something if you tried harder." She didn't care that she'd been caught eavesdropping. She didn't care about the stunned looks her parents gave her. *What kind of husband was he?*

"Hannah!" her mother reprimanded her.

Greg stood up. His voice came out as a shout, words rushing out like a downpour. "I would give *anything* to have her back. I would give anything to go back in time and tell her to wait for her water. To tease her. Kiss her. Pull her down next to me. Anything to hold her long enough for the train to fall without her. You think that I didn't try? You think I don't care? I . . . LOVED . . . HER."

Hannah hung her head. How could she accuse the man Dinah finally gave her heart to? She held her head in her hands. Something had to stop this crazy banging in her head.

"It's okay, Greg," Hannah's mom said, circling his back with the palm of her hand. It was the motion she used when she was helping her kids relax and go to sleep. "We know you did all you could."

Greg shook his head. "I tried. I tried. I laid her down and started giving her CPR until someone grabbed me by the arm and pulled me away. But I took her, I held on to her, I held on to Dinah, all the long, long way to the hospital. And I prayed for her the whole way."

His voice went hard. "They pronounced her dead on arrival." He paused, and shook his head. "I should've gotten the water."

Hannah lifted her head, her view blurred. She wanted to be mad at Greg. He'd been there. He could've saved her, couldn't he? Someone must have been able to save her. God could have rescued her.

"Greg, it's not your fault. It was a freak thing, and a tragedy. But it wasn't your fault." Mrs. Connor laid a comforting hand on Greg's shoulder. But Greg shrugged it off.

"Hannah," Greg said, "come and join us."

She released the banister she'd been clinging to for dear life and stiffly joined him on the couch.

"I understand if you're mad at me. I'm mad at me, too. Your aunt loved you so much," he said.

Hannah nodded. That, she knew.

The elder Connors offered more words of comfort, shed more tears, and began discussing plans for a funeral. Hannah knew they were talking, could somehow hear what they were saying, but she felt transferred to a rail bridge in Africa. She watched her aunt fall. She watched her struggle for life. She watched her die. She could see herself racing down the ravine, seeing people lying in the dirt, looking carefully at each one in search of her aunt. She could hear her aunt screaming. *Why hadn't she been there? Why hadn't she prayed? Why had God abandoned them all?*

chapter 15

The setting was soft and moony, muted beyond distinctive colors. Hannah walked onto the front porch and found it filled with yellow roses, huge blossoms covering every inch, with the paled sun catching every drop of dew on their delicate petals. They had to be from him—her secret admirer. She looked around expectantly. Where was he? He had to be around somewhere. There he was, holding a single yellow rose in his hand, extended it out toward her . . . beckoning her toward him. It looked like . . . Galvin?

Beep. Beep. Beep.

Hannah reached over to shut off her alarm. *What day was today? What did that dream mean?* Through barely opened eyes she looked around the room for a clue, her eyes settling on a black mark on her wall.

Yesterday.

Journaling.

Throwing the pen.

Dinah.

The words came like painful snapshots. Her stomach clenched. Is this what every day was going to be like from now on? Waking up in disbelief? Sleeping numbed to the sadness only to wake up with it smacking her in the face?

She plodded down the stairs to the bathroom to splash water on her face. She needed to quickly get out of this semi-dreamy state into reality. What was she thinking? How could she be having dreams about her admirer when her family was in such turmoil? With Dinah gone, how could she be dreaming about Galvin?

● ● ●

The entire Connor family sat in their regular church pew. Hannah knew they all watched the pastor through bleary eyes. Her chest felt weighted with tears yet she refused to cry in public. Tame tears escaped, but she held back the sobs that tore at her. Pastor Mitchell, in all his gentleness, announced to the congregation the news of Dinah's death, although the majority of the members of First Community Church had already heard through the prayer chain.

Mom had hoped attending church would bring the family a small comfort. She'd told Hannah as the two had prepared breakfast for the rest of the family that there would be rest in the house of God. Dad had wanted stability—something normal, something routine.

Micah was hard to read. Hannah glanced at him during the offertory; he stared ahead—red eyes glazed and hard. He'd barely said a word about Dinah, although Hannah could see his face was splotched and swollen from crying. Rebekah sniffed into a handkerchief throughout the service. Daniel kept wiping his eyes. The twins had wanted to sit with the family today instead of going to little kids' church. They sat, one on each side of Hannah, drawing pictures on the back of their bulletins.

She looked down at Elijah's drawing at one point to see him sketching a gravestone. She took it away from him and crumpled it up, willing Pastor Mitchell to finish his sermon. She wanted to get out of here. She didn't feel peace or stability—she felt cramped and suffocated. She couldn't even hear the words above her loud thoughts.

Did this really happen?

Yes, she kept reminding herself.

It's true. She's not coming back.

Could she have done anything to prevent it? And if God could allow this to happen, what else was He capable of? She squeezed Sarah Ruth's hand protectively. *Please don't take anyone else,* she prayed.

● ● ●

Beef stew and potatoes were a Connor family favorite, but today it mostly stayed untouched.

Will things ever be the same? Hannah couldn't fathom normal. She silently cleaned up after lunch, scraping the remains of her untouched plate into the garbage disposal.

"Hannah, are you doing all right?" Mrs. Connor touched Hannah's arm.

Am I all right? Are any *of us all right?* What kind of question was that? Hannah shrugged. "As good as can be expected, I suppose." She turned on the garbage disposal.

"Do you want to talk?" her mom asked when it stopped running.

Hannah shook her head. She often found comfort sharing her thoughts with her mom, but today she just wanted to pretend the whole mess never happened. She didn't want to think or cry or mourn or talk. She just wanted to escape. Yet she felt the responsibility to be there for her family. After all, her parents were grieving, too. Someone had to keep the house together.

"Thanks, Mom," she said. "I'm fine."

The phone rang and Hannah picked it up. "Hello?"

"It's me, Jacie. How are you doing?"

"I'm fine," she repeated. She noticed her mother watching her out of the corner of her eye.

"We were wondering if you wanted to go to the Copperchino with us—just to talk and stuff."

"I don't think I should leave my family today, but thanks."

Hannah's mom signaled to Hannah to put the phone down.

"Hold on a minute," Hannah told Jacie.

Mrs. Connor wiped her hands on a dishtowel. "Why don't you go out with your friends? It will be good for you. This house is like a tomb."

"But what about the dishes?" Hannah didn't really want to go. Her friends would make her talk about her aunt, and she felt like hiding under the covers of her bed, sleeping or reading or just forgetting everything that happened.

"Rebekah and I can take care of them," Mrs. Connor said. "Just go."

● ● ●

Hannah felt an odd mix of comfort and agony as the group sat talking in the Copperchino. Being in this place reminded her of Aunt Dinah. Only a couple weeks ago, they'd all sat around chatting with her in these same seats. She could almost smell her aunt's light perfume. What had they talked about? Baby clothes. Solana's experiment. Nothing of consequence. It seemed almost silly. There must have been so much to say and they talked about Solana flirting with Galvin. Why something so insignificant? The thought pained her.

"Too bad the cute coffee guy isn't here today," Solana said, looking around for something to say.

Hannah glanced at the petite college-aged girl behind the counter. She'd never seen her before. But with her short, sassy hairstyle she looked a little like Aunt Dinah.

"How's your family doing, Hannah?" asked Becca, leaning her crutches against the side of the chair. The friends had already gone through the questions of how Hannah was doing, only to be rewarded with one-word answers.

Hannah shrugged. "Okay." What could she say? Rebekah had locked herself in her room. Micah continued to play computer games for hours on end. The twins would ask silly questions about death. *Is Aunt Dinah watching us now? Will God let her come back to visit? Can I send her a letter in heaven?*

"Is there anything we can do?" asked Tyler.

"Whatever you do, don't bring any more casseroles." She knew her friends meant well, but there was nothing to do. The only thing she wanted was for Aunt Dinah to walk in the door with her chirpy "Hi, everyone!" But no one could make that happen. "Maybe if we talked about something else."

Her friends exchanged looks.

"Well, I applied to Copper Ridge Community College," Tyler said, "and UNC. Not happily. But I'll do what I have to, I guess."

"Have you decided on a school yet, Jacie?" asked Hannah.

"Not really. But I'm looking into a really good art school in San Francisco."

"I bet your dad would like having you close by," Becca said.

"I hope so. I haven't told him yet." Jacie bit into her bagel.

The conversation seemed forced and stilted, like everyone was reading from a script titled "Normal Conversation."

"But I've been praying about it to see if this is where God

wants me to be," Jacie said. "I'd appreciate it if the rest of you would pray about it, too."

"Sure," said Becca.

Tyler nodded.

Hannah wanted to. The Good Hannah would. The Good Hannah would say that God would show Jacie where to go in His perfect timing and she only needed to trust Him. But Hannah couldn't make herself say it. She didn't believe it. Face it, if God would let someone as good and loving as Aunt Dinah die, why would He care about where Jacie went to school? Or where any of them went to school? The Good Hannah wouldn't think like that. But the Good Hannah didn't seem to be around right now. And the new, I-Don't-Care Hannah reared her head.

"I can't promise anything," Hannah said.

She wanted the best for Jacie. She wanted the best for all her friends, but she couldn't believe that God wanted the best for them. Did God want the best for anyone?

She looked at the brace on Becca's leg. "I'm not sure God cares about stuff like that." She looked at the circle of friends around her, from blank face to blank face. "It doesn't really seem like God is on any of our sides. Tyler's dream of going to CU was crushed, Becca's dream of basketball this year was snapped shut, Solana lost Ramón, and . . ." She looked to Jacie. "Why would a God who cared allow you to have such an empty relationship with your dad? All the good things in our lives got stamped out."

"I hate having the problem with my knee," Becca said. "And I hate giving up basketball even more. But I don't feel that God is against me."

"Same here," said Tyler. "It makes me wonder what God is up to, though. Why He allowed all these things to happen."

Hannah traced the design on her mug with her fingertip. "I'm not sure if I believe in God anymore."

Jacie nodded, her voice small. "I believe in God, but I really am doubting He loves or cares about *me*. If this accident shows how He cares, I'm not so sure—"

"You don't mean that," Tyler said to both of them.

Jacie looked into her lap. Hannah answered. "I don't know. I'm not sure what I believe anymore. It's just . . ."

What was it?

But words poured out anyway, like they'd been stuffed behind a dam until it had to burst. "It's just the God I believed in doesn't do stuff like this. He doesn't take away someone who is so loved and so good, for no reason. He doesn't kill someone and the baby she's carrying just because I didn't pray enough. What kind of God is that?"

"The accident didn't happen because you didn't pray enough," Tyler said.

"Then why was it? If God is so powerful why would He let this happen? And if He's so good why would He let this happen? I don't know this God anymore." Her voice softened. "And I don't think I want to know Him."

"I wish I knew what to say," said Becca, after a pause. "I do believe God cares for us, but I don't have any idea why He would allow this to happen."

Hannah bit her lip. "She was on a missions trip. She was delivering medicine to people who were dying. She didn't even get there," she said, more to herself than anyone else. The whole thing was sometimes so unreal. Unfathomable. There wasn't any sense to it. No sense at all. God could have kept her from going back into that car. God could have sent angels to hold up the bridge while it crossed. God could have caught Dinah when she fell and allowed her to be safe. Now that would've been a miracle that would've driven people *to* God, instead of away. What a great story that would've been of God's power. *You really blew that one, God.*

Jacie's soft words came next. "I guess I wish the old Hannah were here to give you . . . and me . . . the right answers." Jacie's face looked odd. Pale. Pinched. But not something Hannah could care about right now.

The old Hannah. The Good Hannah. She wasn't the same person, and she probably never would be. What would she have told a friend last week if this had happened to them? *God's still in control. You just need to trust His reasons. Maybe He loved your aunt so much He wanted her all to Himself. She's in a better place.* Hannah felt sick to her stomach to the point she could taste the bile in her mouth. People at church had said those words as they shoved Saran-wrapped pies into her hands. Why do people think they can fill the barrenness of grief with stupid words and sweet desserts? The thought of those words infuriated her. *They have no idea.* How dare someone minimize her pain! How dare God be so selfish that He take away someone that meant the world to her just so He could have her all to Himself!

"Hannah, are you okay?" asked Becca.

Hannah looked down at her hands, clenched and sweaty on her lap. She felt the redness in her face. "I'm sorry. I was just thinking."

"About Dinah?" said Jacie.

"Sort of." She might as well spill it. "About why God would do something like this. Before I'd have a whole slew of answers, but right now, none of them is good enough."

Death: *When nothing matters.*

● ● ●

Mrs. Connor seemed to be drowning in photos when Hannah opened the door after Jacie dropped her off.

"What are you doing?" she asked.

"Looking for photos for the memorial service," her mom

answered. "And you know me, I start looking through all these boxes of photos and I'm lost somewhere down memory lane."

Hannah and her mom were alike in that way. They both loved photographs. In the living room alone, there were probably 20 framed pictures of family members—many of which Hannah had taken herself.

"Do you remember this?" Mrs. Connor held out an aged photo. "You were so young when Aunt Dinah took you to the beach."

Hannah looked at herself: A pudgy, blonde baby covered in sand looked out at the water with both excitement and awe. A very young Aunt Dinah kneeled beside her, holding the sand bucket and pail.

Mrs. Connor shook her head. "You two would have such a good time together. I think that's why Dinah wanted a little girl. She remembered how much she loved being with you."

They flipped through the next few photos: Dinah dressing up Hannah like a little bride for a costume party, Dinah and Hannah making cookies—both with flour splotches on their faces, Dinah holding a young Micah and Hannah on her lap, reading them a story.

"There are so many photos of her and me," said Hannah.

"I know. I didn't realize we took so many." Mrs. Connor straightened a few stacks of pictures in front of her. "And what's amazing is that the relationship never weakened. You two have always had a special bond."

Her mom said the sentence in present tense, as though nothing had changed in the last few days. Hannah flipped through more pictures, thinking there would never be another photo taken of her and Dinah. These were all she had.

"Do you want to help me pick some out?" Mom asked.

"No," I-Don't-Care Hannah said. She excused herself up to her room. She didn't want to plan a memorial service. She didn't want to journal. She didn't want to talk to God. She didn't know what she wanted to do except get rid of this concrete statue that seemed to be poured into her body. She wanted to just let it crack. Let it go. But who would understand? Who could handle it? And what would she say?

Whenever she didn't know how to express herself, there was always one person who could get it out of her, who could hug her and ask all the right questions and look at her with all the understanding in the world that would make it all come out. Even when Hannah didn't know what it was. One special person.

But that person was gone . . . and she was never coming back.

The nausea rose back into Hannah's mouth. She couldn't swallow the taste.

See what You did, God? You took away the one person I could talk to about this. See what You did?

chapter 16

Hannah's parents had told her she could skip school on Monday, but she needed to get out of the house. She needed something normal. And what could be more "normal" than lockers and homework and mushy ravioli for lunch?

Hannah twirled the combination of her locker, thinking of things she needed to get done. She'd have to put in a lot of studying for her English test on Friday, plus there was big project due in history next week. It was enough to keep her mind off her aunt, and that was the point.

"I'm surprised you showed up today," a female voice behind her said.

Kassidy stood inches away in a tight denim skirt, her hands folded across her ample chest. *How did Kassidy know about Dinah?*

Kassidy continued, "I knew you skipped out early on the game Friday. I'd just been coming over to say hi. How rude of you to duck out. You weren't avoiding me, were you?"

Hannah stared at the girl in stunned silence. *How could anyone—even Kassidy—be so insensitive?*

Kassidy seemed unaffected by Hannah's widened eyes. "It was just a picture. Sheesh, girl, get over it. Your reputation isn't *that* precious!"

"What?" Hannah sputtered.

"You still expect people to believe you're not interested in Galvin? Oh my, you are pathetic." Kassidy swung a folded copy of Friday's photo spread in her hand like a pendulum.

Hannah watched the paper, almost hypnotized by the sway. She couldn't even focus enough on it to soak in what Kassidy was saying. And then she remembered. The photo. That horrible photo that had ruined her photo spread.

And she thinks that's a big deal? Hannah could've laughed at the absurdity of it all. Friday's disappointment seemed like another world ago—another Hannah ago. And the pain of that day was like a paper cut compared to the agony of a crushed heart. At this point she didn't care if she'd been caught shoplifting cupcakes wearing only her underwear. Her entire world had shattered, and Kassidy thought she was upset about a stupid picture?

Hannah's shoulders stiffened. She was tired of this. Why could horribly mean people like Kassidy live happily day to day, while perfectly wonderful people like Dinah die without even being given a chance to fight it? She'd had enough of Kassidy's ploys, sarcastic comments, and rude behavior. It was done. Good Hannah was gone. She wasn't going to go on being nice and sweet and understanding. If this is the way Kassidy wanted to be, fine. Then Kassidy would get what she deserved.

"Let me tell you something, Kassidy," she said in a voice that was stronger than her own. "You're a self-centered, overly made-up, slutty loser."

Kassidy's mouth fell open. But the words felt good to Hannah. It was as though the anger and frustration inside her suddenly had the tiniest bit of relief—like someone opening the valve of an overly inflated life raft. The feelings—and the words—continued to flow. The anger, the hurt, the fear. All in Kassidy Jordan's pretty, shocked face.

"Guess what. You're too annoying, dull, and plastic to get Galvin's attention. He's got better taste than to be taken in by your pathetic attempts to manipulate him. He's got the brains to see through your façade and reject you flat on your rear end. Face it, without the makeup and revealing clothes, you are nothing but a conniving and rude wanna-be."

Relief: *Letting it all out.*

Kassidy stared at her, snapped her still-open mouth shut, opened it, then shut it again. She turned on her heel and walked away.

Hannah watched her go. *See, God? That's what You get. If You're not going to play by the rules, don't expect me to either.*

● ● ●

"You did what?" Jacie asked.

"I told her off. And I don't think I was very nice about it," Hannah said. She half-smiled at the memory. Even though she felt a little guilty about the whole thing, she'd been anxiously waiting for lunch so she could tell the whole group.

"That's so weird." Solana took a big gulp of milk. "I can't even picture it. I mean you're perfect, holy Hannah."

"I don't know where that Hannah is right now," Hannah said, "so you're going to have to make do with this one."

Tyler was still shaking his head. "I overheard her telling one of her friends about it after my trig class. I just thought she was being overdramatic as usual."

"If you guys knew the way she's been treating me these last

couple weeks, you would understand," Hannah said. "She's done everything to make my life miserable, including that picture. I can guarantee it."

"You don't have to explain," said Becca. "It's Kassidy Jordan. We all know about her character. The point is, we thought we knew *yours*, too."

But maybe I've always been like this, Hannah thought. *But it's always been hidden under who I was supposed to be. And maybe I just didn't want to make my parents mad, or make God mad, and maybe I wanted people to like me. And now, I just don't care.*

Hannah wiped her fingers with a napkin. "So you think I shouldn't have said what I did."

"I don't know. It doesn't really matter. I'm sure it's forgivable," Becca said.

Hannah wadded up the napkin absentmindedly. "Right now, I'm not sure of anything." She wondered what her aunt would have thought of her behavior. Was she up in heaven watching her, shaking her head in disappointment? *I always thought better of you, Hannah.*

"I just hope she and her friends don't strike a vendetta against you," said Solana.

Hannah shrugged. "I really don't care. High school only lasts another eight months. What's that in the whole scheme of my life? Dinah's gone forever."

● ● ●

"And as you'll see on your chart of elements, there are only two elements that fit this criteria. . . ." Dr. Hanson droned on and on. Lecture days in chemistry were even worse than experiment days.

Hannah doodled on her paper. *McKenzie Joy.* McKenzie means "Favored One," Aunt Dinah had said. A lot of good that did her. His favor didn't come through that time. *And maybe it never did. Maybe if we're going to go places in life, we go there our-selves.* She thought about Jacie's dress at Raggs by Razz. The girls hadn't settled themselves in front of the store window to pray that the dress would somehow drop into their laps; they went inside and came up with a plan to get it. In fact, she hadn't prayed about it at all. And then, when she'd prayed about Tyler's college acceptance, Jacie's dad visiting, or Becca's leg in the waiting room of the hospital, everything had turned out wrong. What was the point? Maybe she just needed to take control of her own life instead of waiting for some God—who may or may not care—to do it for her.

She felt a sharp tap on her shoulder and reached back for a wadded note.

Hannah,
    I was really sorry to hear about your aunt.
Do you want to go have coffee after school and
talk about it?
    —G

Hannah twirled her pen through her fingertips, trying to think of an appropriate response. Although she appreciated Galvin's sentiments, she didn't really trust him. Was this his way of getting her on a date? The scene from her dream flickered in her mind and then fizzled out.

Galvin,
    Thanks for the offer. But I need to be with
my Brio friends right now.
    —H

She managed to take semi-comprehensible notes for the rest of class. Although, if you'd asked her once the lecture was over what it was about, she wouldn't be able to tell you a single thing. She filled her backpack slowly as the other students trickled out of the room. Galvin remained, watching her.

"I'm glad your friends are taking care of you. I just wanted to offer," he said.

Hannah nodded. "And I really did appreciate it."

"If you want, I can join you all when you go out." He followed her out of the room.

"I don't think so." She tried to hurry her pace, indicating that the conversation was over.

"Or maybe we could talk some other time. Like Friday."

"No." She stopped and turned around to face him. She'd dreamed of him, yet she was annoyed by him. He didn't know her—not really. And why did he keep trying to ask her out after she'd made it very clear she wasn't interested? Was it all about the conquest? The challenge? A rage rolled up inside her, but she held it back. Whatever Galvin deserved, he didn't deserve her anger unfurled.

"Listen, Galvin," she started. "I know you mean well. But I still feel like you're just trying to go on a date with me, and I don't appreciate it."

She'd never known herself to be so blunt before, and she kind of liked watching his response.

"Well . . . I kinda hoped . . . but I did want to help you through this." He stumbled through his words.

"You're fun. And smart. And I know a number of girls who'd like to date you, but I'm not one of them. And, frankly, it's getting a little annoying," she said.

"I thought you liked me—at least a little," he said.

"I think I did for a while, but I'm over it now."

"Oh."

"I'll see you around." She turned back and was caught up in the tide of students.

"Hannah, wait!" Galvin grabbed onto her backpack. "There's one more thing I need to tell you."

Oh, no. Please don't confess your undying love. "What is it?"

"You might not care anymore, but I thought you should know—"

"Galvin, I really need to get to my next class."

"This will just take a second. I overheard Kassidy talking to her friends about the picture of us in your photo spread."

Her curiosity was piqued. "What did she say?"

"Aaron exchanged it for her."

"Aaron Pritchard?" Why would the sports editor do a thing like that?

"Apparently she could get him and his band a chance to play at her dad's club. And she said she'd guarantee it if he swapped out a picture for her."

Well, that solved the mystery.

"Thanks for letting me know. You're a good friend."

Galvin looked sheepish. "Are you sure I'm not a good friend you'd like to hang out with?"

Hannah had to laugh at his persistence. "I'm sure. Thanks again, Galvin."

She didn't wait for him to say anything else, but headed to her next class.

Despair: *When nothing else—betrayal, vengeance, romance, or persistence—matters in the least.*

chapter 17

"Here you go." The coffee guy placed the drinks in front of each of the friends. *You know you come to a restaurant a lot when the server doesn't even have to ask which drink belongs to whom,* Hannah mused. He handed her a honey dispenser for her tea.

"Thanks," she said.

The Copperchino seemed the safest haven to hide out. No one felt like doing much except sitting around. Even talking had become unnecessary.

Solana clinked a spoon against her glass mug to get everyone's attention. "I'm officially announcing that, as of today, the Galvin Parker experiment is terminated."

Tyler applauded politely. "And what were your findings, Professor Luz?"

"That I need to grow up and get over Ramón before I start flirting with other guys."

Hannah's eyes widened.

"And you may only hear this come out of my mouth once, Hannah, so you better appreciate it," Solana said. "But you were right. I was using Galvin as a game, and I didn't really care about him."

"And the grinch grows a heart!" Tyler said.

"I am not a grinch," Solana said. "But I was pretty emotionless, or at least trying to be."

"No more queen-beeing?" said Becca.

"My stinger has been cut off," Solana smiled wryly.

"Well, I guess he's all yours, Hannah," said Jacie.

"No, thanks. Kassidy Jordan can have him," Hannah said. She was glad she hadn't told anyone about the dream.

"Any other experiments lined up?" asked Tyler.

Jacie pointed her eyes toward the counter. "You always thought the coffee guy was cute."

"I think I'm done for a while," Solana said. "I miss Ramón. I miss him a lot. And I need to deal with that first."

"Then you need to e-mail him and let him know," said Hannah.

"Wait a minute." Becca set down her mug. "Now you're encouraging Solana to be in contact with Ramón? You were all about her getting over him."

"And I don't think I better e-mail him anyway. Not after that message he sent," said Solana.

"Your response to his note is what makes me think you need to contact him again. You don't have to beg him to take you back, but let him know you were hurt and wrote back without thinking about it. Tell him you still like him and that in a few months when he's sorted through everything he needs to sort through, you'd like to hear from him."

"Really? But he's not a Christian, remember?"

"Neither are you. Remember?" Hannah shrugged. "Just my humble opinion."

"I don't know." Solana twisted a dark lock of hair between her fingers. "What if he thinks I'm pining after him?"

"You are pining after him," said Becca.

"But I don't want him to know that. I'll scare him away," Solana argued back.

"But you can't leave it like it is now. He thinks you hate him," said Jacie.

"Yeah. Remember, you're having the time of your life right now," Tyler reiterated the note. "You forgot he'd even left."

Solana dropped her head into her open palms and rocked her head back and forth. "I can't believe I told him that," she said, her voice muffled.

"So my vote is with Hannah. You write him a short note and let him do what he wants with it," said Jacie.

"I'm there, too," agreed Tyler. "You can't just sit around and hope he comes back. You need to be proactive."

"You're one to talk," said Hannah.

"What's that supposed to mean?" said Tyler. "I don't want to date Ramón."

"You haven't done anything to try to get yourself into CU-Boulder."

"I was turned down. I tried, thank you very much," Tyler said.

"But what about retaking your SATs and reapplying? It seems like you could at least call an admissions counselor and see why you weren't accepted, and then you'll know how to better your application."

"Oh." Tyler threw up his hands. "Now you come up with the brilliant ideas."

Hannah smirked. "If I'm the brilliant one, maybe *I'll* be able to get in." The heartrending sadness took one step back.

"Personally, I think reapplying is a great idea," Solana said. "What about this all being in God's hands and leaving it up to Him?"

Hannah looked past Solana to a landscape painting on the wall. Ducks circled a pond in the middle of a meadow. It wasn't a particularly good painting, but it kept her eyes off of Solana's. "I'm having second thoughts about that. Maybe some things God doesn't really care about, so we need to take care of them ourselves."

"No, no, no," Becca said, wagging her head emphatically. "God cares about everything that happens to us."

Tyler jumped in. "You're way off base on this one, Hannah."

Hannah stared at her hands in her lap.

"Look. I'm not trying to stomp on you. But I think God permeates everything we do. He wants to be with us *in* everything we do."

"Well, don't we have to do something?" Hannah asked. "I mean, you can't get into CU if you don't get great grades. God's not going to zap those into being for you."

Tyler nodded. "I agree. We do our part; God does His part. We certainly can't just sit around hoping God's going to bring answers for tests into our heads if we've never studied. The Christian life is a partnership—with God leading. The non-Christian life is a life people live alone and lead by themselves."

Hannah squirmed. Nothing made sense in her brain anymore. Who was God? What was He? How did He play into their lives? She didn't want to get into it. She turned to Tyler. "I can help you study for the SATs if you want to take them again," she said.

"I can coach you on the science section," volunteered Solana.

"Cool. Who knows what could happen?" Tyler looked more excited than he had been in over a week.

"Okay, okay," said Becca. "This is all fine and dandy, so I have to ask: Do you think God made my knee get hurt?"

Hannah swallowed. She hated eating her own words. "I've changed my mind. Now I think it was just a freak accident—

which brings me to the next thing I wanted to talk to you all about."

Jacie leaned forward. "We're all ears."

"Why should the kids at the Community Center have to miss out on hiking just because of a clumsy Green Mountain player?"

"They shouldn't. But I can't really lead a group like this." Becca motioned toward her knee brace.

"But we could help. And maybe Solana's uncle can lend you a horse. You could still *ride* on a trail, couldn't you?" Hannah suggested.

"That's a great idea," said Solana. "I'm sorry I didn't think of it myself."

"But what if you were right the first time? What if this all happened because God wanted to force me to spend more time with Him and less time being busy? I thought about it after you left the other day. And even though I didn't like it, it sorta made sense," Becca said. "I don't know what He wants me to do."

"The way I see it, if God is as powerful as we've been told and He really doesn't want something to happen, then it won't." Hannah thought of the bridge buckling in Kenya. "He'd stop it somehow." She took a sip of tea and continued. "But what if God isn't as in control as I thought? Maybe not everything has a purpose or a reason. So we might as well make the best of what we have."

It felt good and bad to say that, freeing in a sense, and painful, too. She'd believed that about God her whole life—a God who always planned the best for her. Now what? If she didn't believe that about God, was life all up to her?

Tyler and Becca exchanged glances. Tyler set his mug down on the table. "I agree sometimes God lets us make our own choices, but I still think He's deeply involved in our lives. You almost make it sound like God doesn't care at all."

Hannah shrugged. "I don't know anymore. It's really hard to reconcile how all this . . ." She paused, remembering Uncle Greg's story. ". . . could happen if God really were involved. I either have to believe God doesn't care or He wasn't powerful enough to do anything about it. Some days I think He's heartless, some days I think He has limited control, other days I don't know." She looked at her friends' somber faces. "Today's one of those days."

"But we don't know the bigger picture God has in store," said Becca. "I don't think God killed your aunt, but I have to believe that He's still sovereign—and He's still good. You've said it yourself over and over that we can't understand God's ways. We just can't. We're too small. And we can't put God into a box that fits our own understanding."

We can't put God into a box. Dinah had said that, too. *He won't fit,* she'd said. The reiteration caught her off guard. "Maybe that's true," she responded. Her words came slow and plodding. "But would you be able to say that if your brother died while doing his volunteer work at college?"

Becca's face went blank. Solana intercepted the conversation. "I think what Hannah means is, well, even if it is right what you say about God, it hurts too much to believe it right now."

Hannah nodded. How funny. Of all the people in this group to speak right from Hannah's heart, it was the non-Christian. For a moment, she could put herself in Solana's shoes. She understood unbelief, the feeling of not knowing what is really true, when it seems like everyone around you has it all figured out.

"I don't understand it, either," Jacie said, her eyes filled with tears.

Hannah smiled sadly as she squeezed Jacie's hand. "Thanks." She remembered the other thing she wanted to say to the group.

"And, Jacie, if God is good at all, He planned you. Despite the sin involved, you're an incredible person. So I don't care whether it was a mistake or not."

"Thanks."

The group chatted for the next hour or so. Hannah noticed Jacie giving her funny looks, as though she wanted to say something but didn't know what. She probably wanted to tell her that God was still ultimately in control, but Hannah didn't want to hear it right now. It felt good to take charge of her own life and not leave everything up to God and a few prayer journals. Maybe it wasn't "God's will" that Tyler didn't go away to college. But maybe God just didn't give a rip, so why not go for it?

● ● ●

The group was heading for the door when Hannah caught up with Solana. *One more conversation I need to have*, she reminded herself.

"Solana, I just wanted to say I'm . . . really sorry."

"For what? Hannah, I meant it when I said I was over Galvin. I was never really that interested in him in the first place. It's okay," Solana said, as she worked the combination on her bike lock.

"I mean, I'm sorry for the way I've treated you in the past."

"What do you mean?" Solana looked up.

"I know I've been judgmental toward you, even though I didn't mean to be. I really thought I had all the answers, and I wanted to give those answers to you. Because I cared about you—really. But I think somewhere along the line, *telling* you all the answers became more important than caring about *you*."

Solana looked at her for a moment, as if deciding on Hannah's sincerity. "Thanks. I know you had good intentions."

"Now I know I don't have all the answers and I realize how annoying I must have been."

"Sometimes," Solana smirked.

"So can you forgive me for being a pain?"

"Of course. That's what friends do."

"What? Forgive or be pains?" Hannah teased.

"Both, I think," Solana said. "But I'm forgiving you. You know, you're all right, Hannah Connor."

The two stood in silence for a long minute. But Hannah didn't really want to move. For the first time, she felt bonded to Solana. Like she understood her. It wasn't about proving anything to her or being right. It was just okay to look at each other through a bike rack and know they were friends. She didn't have to come up with reasons why Solana and Ramón shouldn't be together. She could just feel bad that not being together hurt Solana so much. She opened her mouth to ask about Ramón, but Solana's words came first.

"Hannah, can I ask you something?"

It's always a bad sign when someone asks if they can ask you something instead of just saying it, but Hannah nodded. She really didn't have anything to hide.

"Do you still believe in God? And in heaven and . . . well, everything you used to believe in?"

Hannah sighed. "I honestly don't know what I believe. I know I need to sort things out. My faith isn't as simple as it used to be. And, frankly, right now I'm pretty mad at God."

"But I guess you have to believe in someone in order to be mad at them."

"Yeah," Hannah said. For some reason, Solana's words made her feel better. Her faith wasn't out the window. She didn't want her faith to be gone—she'd clung to it so tightly for so long that it was like having a security blanket being taken away. But she also didn't want to hold onto a blanket that was meaningless.

"So what are you going to do now? Still go to church and stuff?"

"I'll still go to church. My parents will insist on it." Hannah shook her head. "It's funny, really. Even though I feel like stuffing God into the trash compactor, my mom has grown even closer to Him. I can see it on her face. She finds so much comfort in reading the Bible now—and the Scriptures are only making me more angry. I don't get it." Hannah shifted from one leg to the other, wishing that would arrange her thoughts. "I think I just need some time. And not forced time, like praying for an hour every night or trying to read through the entire Bible. I can't tell you what's next, but I think I'm just going to go on with life. And if God's around, He knows where to find me."

A slow smile spread across Solana's face. "Y'know, I kinda like you when you don't have the answers."

Hannah's lip curled up into a half-smile. "Then I think you're going to start liking me a lot more." She started working on her own bike lock, next to Solana. "I'll see you tomorrow."

"Great," Solana said. "Oh, and Hannah?"

Hannah turned to see a face she'd never seen on Solana before—something earnest and sincere.

"I'd really be interested in hearing what comes about. I mean, what answers you do get."

"Really?" Was this the Solana she'd known for the past year who'd never wanted anything to do with God?

"Yeah. Really."

Weirdness: *That conversation.*

chapter 18

Hannah biked down to the park before dinner. She didn't care if Kassidy and her friends were there. She wouldn't even acknowledge them. She just needed some time by herself. Taking charge of life seemed to help her friends, and it made her happy to see them feel better. But it left something lacking in her. For the umpteenth time in the past couple days, she wished she could talk to Dinah.

The park was empty, except for the occasional squirrel gathering the last of the winter's supply. A blanket of leaves drifted onto the pond. She sat down on a bench and watched them spin in the water and the wind.

For the first time that day she realized how cold it was. Cold enough that it might snow that night. She buried her nose into the collar of her coat. *I don't care. I don't care about anything. I don't know how You could do this, God. This is Dinah, who loved*

You and wanted to serve You and was on a missions trip. What more do You want?

She paused.

The wind blew cold silence into her ears.

Forget it. I don't care. Just forget it.

She didn't even want to hear God. No explanation, no reason He could give her would ever be enough. She didn't even know what she believed. Was there a God? She'd always thought so. He'd always seemed so real. But did this God love her? *Really* love her? *Really* want what was best for her? She remembered Solana's words: *Well, that kind of love I can do without.*

Hannah felt someone's eyes on her. She looked up.

"Hi." It was the coffee guy. *I'm not going to be nice to him. There's no reason.*

"Can I sit down?"

"Suit yourself."

He sat down on the other side of the bench. They both stared out at the water.

"I don't really feel like talking," she said.

Coffee guy nodded. "I understand." He paused. "Your aunt was pretty cool."

"Yeah." She wondered how he'd heard the news. And how did he even know her aunt? Just from the trips to the coffee shop?

He seemed to read her thoughts. "My uncle goes to your church, and he heard through the prayer chain. He knew I know you and your aunt."

It suddenly seemed important to hear what others thought of Aunt Dinah. Almost as if Dinah wasn't obliterated by her death if someone spoke of her life. "Did you ever get a chance to talk to her?"

"I did." He grinned. "In fact, we talked a lot. She usually came in early when she was meeting you for coffee, and she'd sit at the counter. We'd talk about God, philosophy, the arts. She knew a ton."

Hannah smiled. "That's right up her alley. She loves that kind of stuff."

"Sometimes she'd come a half hour early. It was fun. She made me read some of C. S. Lewis's books."

"That's definitely Aunt Dinah."

"She . . . uh . . . she kind of had a soft spot for me."

"Why's that?"

The boy exhaled, his breath leaving a fog lingering in the air. "Because she knew how much I liked you."

Hannah watched the leaves for a minute. She didn't feel embarrassed by what he'd said. More curious. Her aunt knew this, and treated him as though she approved. She needed to know more.

"You told her this?"

"Well, she kind of guessed. So one time she came in early and just asked me what I thought of you. And, well, you know your aunt. She's so easy to talk to. So I spilled it—how I watched you at school and saw you at The Edge. How I knew how you like your tea. How I sent you anonymous flowers."

"You sent the flowers?"

"Yeah."

"Even the ones in Breckenridge?"

"Yep. Even those."

"Why were they always anonymous?"

"I don't think I first intended them to be. But the more I got to know you—hear about you really—the more I respected your stance on courtship. I didn't want to pressure you or disrespect your commitment to God by asking you to change that."

"But you kept sending them."

Coffee guy nodded. "It felt right. I wanted you to feel cared for. I wanted you to feel special. I'm not sure why it was so important, except that I thought it would help you stick to your beliefs if you knew how attractive and valued you were."

"You sound like my aunt," Hannah said.

"She drilled it into me," he joked. " 'You better treat my niece right. She's an amazing girl!' " he mimicked. Hannah laughed.

"And I also thought that if someday we started courting, you'd know I'd pursued you from the first day I laid eyes on you."

"Courting? Do you believe in courting?" She'd never heard a guy at Stony Brook mention the "C" word in reference to himself.

"I think I do. When I heard that's what you believed in, I really admired that you set your standards so high, but never thought that it would be right for me. But as I read more about it, I found that it really makes sense. I talked with my youth pastor about giving up casual dating and he thought it was a great idea. He's been supporting me in that decision for the last year or so."

He gave up dating—because of me?

And he talked about courtship like it is something admirable—not weird, like most people think.

Hannah swallowed. This was her secret admirer. She watched him out of the corner of her eye. Solana had always said he was cute, and he was. "So what made you decide to tell me now?"

"I know . . . great timing, huh, when you've got nothing else on your mind." He exhaled slowly. "The last time your aunt came into the shop, she said that I should talk to you. Not ask you out, but just let you know that it's me who's been sending you the flowers and everything. I insisted I couldn't do it. I told her you'd probably never come into the Copperchino again if I did. And that's when you walked in the door. It was the last thing I said to her."

Hannah nodded. She'd relived her last words to Dinah over and over. *I'll pray for you.* So much for that.

The coffee guy continued, "I came out for a walk today, and when I saw you sitting here it seemed like my chance to honor Dinah in some way, I guess, by doing the last thing she wanted me to do."

Hannah could feel the boy's nervousness as he waited for her response. She didn't feel pressured by him, but her next question seemed terribly awkward. "Can I ask you something then?" she asked.

He nodded.

She flushed with embarrassment, but she had to ask. "What's your name?"

Coffee guy let out a deep laugh. "Grant Andrews."

"It's nice to meet you, Grant."

"You too, Hannah." He grinned. "I've heard so much about you."

"That makes me a little nervous. Aunt Dinah knows a lot about me."

"She did tell me that when you were four she took you to The Gap and you tried to convince the manager that he should stock only blue things, showing him your underwear so he would know what shade."

Hannah covered her face at the memory. "I can't believe she told you that."

"I thought it was adorable," Grant insisted. "She really did think you were the best thing ever. She never said a word about you that was negative. Well," his voice grew somber, "except for that one thing about the parachute pants."

"What?" *The parachute pants?* She jerked her head up to see him grinning at her, and playfully swatted him on the shoulder. "Very funny."

"I couldn't let your head grow too big."

Hannah realized she was smiling, and then immediately felt guilty. Dinah had just died; how could she be smiling over some guy who liked her? That was so small, and this death was so huge. Her face dropped instantly. "I can't believe she's gone."

Grant didn't seem taken aback by her change in mood. It seemed like the most natural thing in the world. "I know. I'm so sorry."

The two returned to staring out at the twirling leaves on the pond. Somehow Hannah felt that Dinah was closer, that she could see them now. So many times her aunt had watched out for her, given her advice, and helped make sense out of things. They even talked about God not making sense. She remembered the last conversation they had. *God is God, whether we understand Him or not. Don't try to fit Him into a box. He won't go there.* If Dinah only knew what God was going to do next, would she still have trusted Him?

"It is sweet that she was trying to get us to talk," she said.

Grant reached into his pocket. "Here's a Kleenex."

Hannah noticed her cheeks were wet with tears. She mopped her face, but the tears kept coming. She wanted to say "thank you," but the lump in her throat wouldn't let anything past. The thought of her aunt talking to a guy—who she knew was a quality guy—about how great Hannah was overwhelmed her. She pictured the conversation. The laughing. The depth. The probing, eager questions her aunt was so good at. And she sobbed. Big, long, hard, deep sobs, that shook her from the core. She leaned into Grant, who put his arms around her, and buried her face into his down jacket. She wanted to regain her poise. She wanted to leave. But the sobs kept coming, and the tears kept falling. And she finally gave in. Grant stroked the top of her head.

"I'm so sorry. I'm so sorry, Hannah," he kept whispering. "It's okay to cry."

She could feel his tears falling on her head, and they brought a strange comfort with them.

● ● ●

Today, after I talked to Grant in the park, I started biking toward the school—just thinking. Sometimes praying, sometimes wondering, sometimes crying. I don't know why Aunt Dinah died, or why You let these things happen. But I don't feel as angry with You right now, just sad. And sad is sometimes harder. I'm sad that I'll never get to hug Dinah again. Sad that I never had the chance to bounce McKenzie on my lap. Sad that I believed in Someone who couldn't or wouldn't help me. Sad that I feel like I'm losing a faith that always seemed like such a huge part of me—that was me. Sad that things will never be the same and I can't do anything about it. Sad that I thought I knew You and now I'm not so sure. But, here I am, still writing You, so I must believe something. I desperately want to believe that I still matter to You—that Dinah mattered to You. And for a moment today, I could. It still didn't make sense, but there was a peace—deep down—that You were still around. I got off my bike to watch the sunset and as I was kicking the piles of leaves on the sidewalk, a big banner rolled toward me, trapped in the wind. The wind died and the banner unfolded at my feet. It must've blown off the school. HAPPY HOMECOMING! it read. I felt like it had *dropped from heaven. Like it was a bit of the party the angels had last Friday.*

Happy Homecoming, Dinah.

Take care of her, God.

● ● ●

Hannah knocked on her parents' bedroom door.

"Come in," her father called.

Her parents were sitting in bed, making notes on a yellow steno pad.

"Hannah. How are you?" Mrs. Connor patted the bed, beckoning her to join them.

Hannah slumped down onto the thick comforter. "I think I'm all cried out."

Mrs. Connor rubbed Hannah's back, and nodded. "I understand that feeling."

"What are you two doing?" Hannah asked.

Her father twirled a pen between his fingers. "Trying to figure out how to do the funeral. Greg's coming over tomorrow and we'll finalize it together."

"We were at the point of trying to think of Dinah's favorite songs," Mrs. Connor explained.

" 'Lord of All Creation,' " said Hannah. "She sang it all the time."

"That's right. She loves that song." Mr. Connor made a note on the yellow paper. "Can you think of any others?"

She listed a few other songs she remembered Dinah humming. Sometimes the two of them would break out in song while they were driving in Dinah's car together. They both could hardly carry a tune but would sing their hearts out, usually ending the song in peals of laughter as the last notes would make even them cringe. Hannah smiled at the memory. They'd had so many wonderful times together. Dinah had given her so much. She wanted to do something to thank her, to honor this woman who'd made such a distinct impact on her life.

"Do you think I could say something at the funeral?"

Her parents looked at each other.

"I think Dinah would have loved that, Hannah," her dad said. "But are you sure you can do it?"

"No. But I want to."

"Then I think that's a good idea," her father said.

"Thanks." She stood up. She'd need to put a lot of thought into what she wanted to say. It had to be good. It had to be good for Dinah. "I should get to bed."

Hannah reached for the doorknob and then thought of something.

"Are you both doing okay?" she asked.

"As good as can be expected," Mrs. Connor said. "So, not very good."

"She was my little sister," her dad said. "She shouldn't have been the first to go." Hannah noticed the glassy look of tears in his eyes.

She walked back to the bed and gave them each a hug. "Good night, Mom. Good night, Dad. I love you."

Hope: *The sparkling something you find in the dark, but you have no idea how you found it.*

chapter 19

People packed out the church sanctuary, squeezed shoulder-to-shoulder in the rows of chairs. *There must be 400 people here,* Hannah thought, as she stood at the front of the church watching people hunt for empty seats. *Everyone loved Dinah.*

She'd been clutching her notes so tightly that the ink had begun to bleed onto her sweaty palms. She switched them to the other hand and picked up the bulletin.

"The Eternal Marriage of Dinah Elizabeth Burkett."

A colored photograph on the front showed Dinah on her wedding day. A bright smile lit up her face, exposing her deep warmth. *She'd be happy with this,* Hannah thought.

After speaking with her parents and Greg, the four decided to plan a wedding-themed funeral, signifying that Dinah was the bride of Christ and now had gone to be with her eternal groom. She'd been nervous that Greg would be opposed to the idea when she brought it up. After all, Dinah had been his bride. But Greg had been the biggest supporter of the idea. "When we got married, Hannah, I knew God was lending me Dinah as my partner here on earth. I didn't know He would take her away this soon. But I know she was never mine to possess, just to love."

The words stuck with Hannah. She'd grown in her respect and admiration for Greg in these last couple of days. He really loved her aunt—still did—and that showed now more than ever.

It would seem unconventional to have a wedding cake at the post-funeral luncheon and to release doves after the ceremony, but no one could say Dinah had ever been conventional.

Dinah's injuries had been mostly internal, so they'd decided on an open casket. Dressed in her wedding gown, Dinah held a bouquet of lilies—her favorite flowers. Hannah had broken into tears as she'd approached the casket the night before. It reminded her of that wedding day just a few months back, when she'd been a bridesmaid for her aunt, carrying a bouquet of lilies of her own. Dinah, always spunky anyway, had been more alive than ever that day. Laughing and teasing and worshiping God—sometimes all in the same sentence.

Now the pastor took his place at the podium and welcomed the attendees. Hannah took a seat between her mother and Greg. A slide show would be next on the agenda, showing Dinah at her best, loving on friends and enjoying every minute of life.

A praise band played a few of her favorite songs and asked the congregation to join them in the celebration. *Dinah would love this.* It was a little too loud for her dad, but completely Dinah's style.

Greg got up to say a few words. He shared numerous stories of his wife, from the time she decided to get back at the youth group by TP-ing *their* cars to when she threw a luau for their two-month anniversary. He shared the time she found an ostrich wandering along a rural road, and how she spent hours walking it from house to house trying to find its owner. Hannah always laughed at the picture of her aunt walking around in her heels and pearls, comforting a lost ostrich. And, with tears, Greg spoke of when she was on an international trip and met a poor family with six children and no father. She took them all out to dinner and shopping at a nearby village, and she continued to correspond with and pray for them.

Then Hannah's dad took the stage, speaking of his little sister's spiritual journey. He'd seen her come through a time of rejecting God, even contemplating an abortion. Dinah's testimony was not a new concept to the people who knew her; she freely shared how far God had brought her. But to hear it from the brother who watched her go through it put it in a new light.

"I know Dinah is with Jesus now," her dad said. "But she is not just now getting to know Him. She's known Him for many years, in ways that I have yet to attain. Although I've been a Christian far longer and have received more biblical education, Dinah had an intimacy with God that exceeds mine. The way she walked with Him and talked with Him, even laughed with Him, is the core of who she was."

Hannah didn't know that her father saw that in Dinah. She'd recognized her closeness—her realness—with God, but she'd never been aware that her dad had, as well.

Finally, Hannah ascended the steps to the podium. Four hundred pairs of eyes stared back. But through her moistened eyes, it only seemed like a blurry sea of grays, blues, and blacks. She cleared her throat:

"Aunt Dinah was my favorite aunt. We had a special relationship, and in some ways she knew me better than anyone. I admired her deeply. I admired her love for people and the passion with which she lived her life. I was inspired by her hunger for God and her beauty that emanated from a gentle and tender heart. She'd seen the worst, and maybe that's why she could love people without judgment. She'd been there, and she knew God's redemption was always bigger. Redemption. I think it must've been one of her favorite words."

The crowd gave a murmur of agreement before Hannah continued.

"When I was little and she babysat for me and my little brothers and sisters, she'd take me outside when the others had gone to sleep. She'd point out to me what she'd call 'Hannah's star'—it was always the brightest star in the sky. She told me that God gave me that star to remind me that I was a princess, and even when things were hard here on earth, that I was still the daughter of a King. And I would be adorned with jewels and a crown." Hannah paused for a minute. "To be honest, right now that's hard to believe. I don't feel loved by God. I don't feel that God has a plan. And I can't say that I believe that right now and be honest—"

She saw Jacie nod in the third row, giving her silent encouragement.

"But something in me still believes that God knows what He's doing. That this wasn't something that happened that totally threw off His plans for each of us or this church or even the people she loved in Kenya." Hannah drew in a deep, shaky breath. "The night before she left on this trip, Aunt Dinah told me, 'Good things are yet to come.' And, for her, I think they have. I pray that each of us, especially me, can learn from her example of love, compassion, and vibrancy—and that we will never be the same having known her."

Tears dropped on the papers in front of her, leaving pools of watery blue ink. She folded up the pages and looked up at the people. The four hundred pairs of eyes.

"We love you, Dinah," she whispered.

Somehow Hannah found herself back at her seat. The pastor offered the time for a few more people to come and read some of Dinah's favorite scriptures. More songs followed. Hannah glanced back at her *Brio* friends. They were dabbing their faces with Kleenexes, but they all gave her "you-did-good" smiles.

● ● ●

"Hannah!" Grant came up to her as she was leaving the burial site. He must have noticed her entourage before he saw her. The *Brio* friends surrounded her like secret service men around the president, protecting her from anyone too sugary sweet.

"Grant! You came. I didn't see you," Hannah said. Grant looked nice—albeit a little uncomfortable—in his dark suit and tie.

Becca, Solana, Tyler, and Jacie each said their hellos. Hannah had told them about her conversation with Grant yesterday, and they all seemed to take the hint that Grant wanted to talk to Hannah alone.

"We'll go help your mom with the little ones," Becca said, as the group headed toward Mrs. Connor's corralling motions, gathering up five-year-olds along the way.

"With all these people, I'd be easy to miss," Grant said. He looked up at her with a soft smile. "I wanted to let you know, I think Dinah would be really proud of what you said today. You sounded just like her."

"Really?" That was the biggest compliment someone could give. She'd always wanted to be like her aunt.

"Definitely. I think she's going to live on in you."

Hannah shook her head. "No one could replace Dinah." She smiled at the thought. "No one else could get away with the stuff she did."

"I think you're a lot more like her than you think. And you already have a head start."

"What do you mean?"

"Dinah didn't start her walk with God until she was your age."

Hannah nodded. It was true. "You knew her pretty well, didn't you?"

"I wouldn't be here unless she impacted my life. I'll miss her a lot."

"I'm glad I said what I said, but . . ." Hannah didn't know why she was admitting this, but, for some reason—maybe because she knew her aunt liked Grant—she felt safe telling him. He nodded his encouragement. "But now I don't know if I believe it. I feel like I'm on this giant swing. One moment I still believe God is in control and one day I'll understand all this, and then the next I'm so overcome with anger I can't even pray. I felt that way at the edge of the grave over there—and then I realized I must be such a hypocrite to say one set of words and then feel another." She took a deep breath. Even she hadn't realized how much was welling up inside her until the valve had been released.

She looked up to see him staring into her eyes. He took her hand and held it in his own. It felt soft and tender. She'd never held a boy's hand before, but this felt surprisingly natural and almost pure. "I've never had someone so close to me die, but I have to think you'll be on that swing for a long time," he said after a minute. "And for what it's worth, I don't think you're a hypocrite. I think you're honest about the way you feel and that's pretty cool."

She nodded and gently slid her hand out of his. Not because she wanted to, but because she realized how many people were mingling around watching. But she wanted to talk to him more. As odd as it was, since she felt like she'd only known Grant for a day, he seemed to be the one person who understood her.

"Do you want to come over to the house for some food? You can meet my parents."

Grant shook his head. "I wish I could, but I need to get back to school."

Hannah nodded. Her *Brio* friends had to get back for the same reason.

"Thanks, Grant."

● ● ●

Tap, tap, tap.

"Come in!" Hannah knew if someone were knocking, it must be her parents. Her siblings just barged in. She knew she should be downstairs helping with dinner. Several of the out-of-town relatives who'd arrived in Copper Ridge for the funeral had come for dinner. The overly perfumed, sickeningly sentimental crowd had made Hannah's stomach queasy. She'd hoped to just be by herself for a while.

Her mother opened the door, holding a small envelope in her hand. "This came for you today."

"Another sympathy card?" Although she'd appreciated people's concern, she'd grown tired of the sappy verses and muted pictures that seemed to have inundated the Connor house.

"I don't think so. It's postmarked from Nairobi."

Hannah's eyes opened so wide they began to tear. *Nairobi. It takes a long time for mail to get from there to here. That means . . .*

Her mother dropped the envelope on Hannah's bed and silently left the room.

chapter 20

Hannah's hands trembled as she tore open the envelope. The note inside was brief—a single piece of paper. A few short lines of her aunt's flowery handwriting graced the page:

Dear Hannah,

We just arrived in Nairobi. It's just as beautiful as I remembered. The entire flight here I sensed God's presence that He was going to do something big on this trip. He gave me such an unbelievable peace—and I thought of you and our conversation about God not making sense. And I prayed for you—that God will always give you the eyes to see Him even in confusion and pain. Life will not always be as easy as it is now; the answers don't come quickly. But God is in this, Hannah. I promise you that. There will be so much to share when I get home!

All my love,
Aunt Dinah

Hannah reread the letter almost a dozen times. She held the paper to her heart and took a deep breath. *Thank You, God.* She knew what she had to do. After selecting a piece of her favorite stationery, she sat down to write:

Dear Aunt Dinah,

I don't know why you had to die. It doesn't seem fair—not for Greg or me or little McKenzie Joy or anyone. I don't know why God would allow this to happen. But you always used to say, 'We live in a fallen world, but God is still sovereign.' And I think I used to believe that. And then, when all this happened with you, I realized I didn't. I don't trust God, sometimes. And, even now, I'm still angry with Him. But I hope you're right—that He is sovereign and good. And I'm not even sure why I hope that, but somewhere inside I do. I may change my mind tomorrow, then back again the next day. I'm trying to believe good things are yet to come, even though it doesn't feel like it right now.

I can't wait to sit down for a nice, long talk when I see you next.

All my love,
Hannah

She carefully folded the note, placed it into an envelope, and tucked it inside the front pocket of her journal.

Life: *Opening your eyes and realizing you're still there.*

FOCUS ON THE FAMILY®

Welcome to the Family!

Whether you received this book as a gift, borrowed it, or purchased it yourself, we're glad you read it. It's just one of the many helpful, insightful, and encouraging resources produced by Focus on the Family.

In fact, that's what Focus on the Family is all about — providing inspiration, information, and biblically based advice to people in all stages of life.

It began in 1977 with the vision of one man, Dr. James Dobson, a licensed psychologist and author of 18 best-selling books on marriage, parenting, and family. Alarmed by the societal, political, and economic pressures that were threatening the existence of the American family, Dr. Dobson founded Focus on the Family with one employee and a once-a-week radio broadcast aired on only 36 stations.

Now an international organization, the ministry is dedicated to preserving Judeo-Christian values and strengthening and encouraging families through the life-changing message of Jesus Christ. Focus ministries reach families worldwide through 10 separate radio broadcasts, two television news features, 13 publications, 18 Web sites, and a steady series of books and award-winning films and videos for people of all ages and interests.

● ● ●

For more information about the ministry, or if we can be of help to your family, simply write to Focus on the Family, Colorado Springs, CO 80995 or call (800) A-FAMILY (232-6459). Friends in Canada may write Focus on the Family, PO Box 9800, Stn Terminal, Vancouver, BC V6B 4G3 or call (800) 661-9800. Visit our Web site — www.family.org — to learn more about Focus on the Family or to find out if there is an associate office in your country.

We'd love to hear from you!

life

love

Want More? Life

Go from ordinary to extraordinary! *Want More? Life* will help you open the door to God's abundant life. You'll go deeper, wider and higher in your walk with God in the midst of everyday challenges like self-image, guys, friendships and big decisions. Spiral hardcover.

Want More? Love

You may ask, "Does God really love me? How can He love me — with all my faults and flaws?" *Want More? Love* is a powerful devotional that shows you how passionately and protectively God loves and cares for you — and how you can love Him in return! Spiral hardcover.

Bloom: A Girl's Guide to Growing Up

You have lots of questions about life. In *Bloom: A Girl's Guide To Growing Up*, your questions are addressed and answered with the honesty youth expect and demand. From changing bodies, to dating and sex, to relationships, money and more, girls will find the answers they need. Paperback.

Brio

It's the inside scoop — with hot tips on everything from fashion and fitness to real-life faith. Monthly magazine.